TALES FROM TRANSFUSION

THE INCLUSION

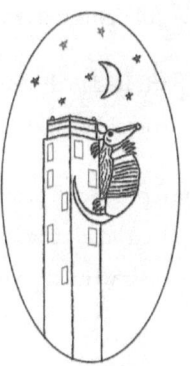

MARLENE TOWER

ISBN: 979-8-9890756-3-8

For anyone who has ever felt like an outsider for refusing to maintain the peace while the peace was exploiting others.

Contents

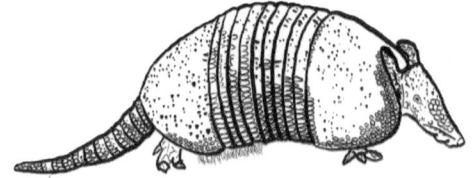

Chapter 1

Wednesday: Eight Days Ago

LIAM TOSSED HIS HOMEMADE red candies in their matching glass bowl. Day one of their FDA inspection complete, he waited in his office to discuss the lab's observations. First observation, "Inspector not greeted with warm welcome. Example: Director made insincere breakfast gesture, followed by sarcastic remark regarding inspector's punctuality." The FDA only documents negative observations.

Yvette called him last night, "I'm going through our internal checklist. So far so good. Is there anything else you can think of to prep the lab?"

"We should already be doing everything. There should be nothing to prep." It was late. Liam did not want to stay up all night working on a problem when the solution already existed.

The mandatory group chat with laboratory admin buzzed non-stop for three minutes. To stave off panic, Liam sent an email. "Off-schedule inspections are common at facilities as large as ours.

We have our policies in place. Our employees are trained to follow policies. Fatima discovered the most recent discrepancy because we have proper backup methods. If our techs are not following policy, or if we have a gap in our error reduction methods, this inspection is our best way of finding it. I know for certain the FDA will not remove our approval to irradiate blood products. Not tomorrow, at least. The most effective thing we can do for our team is to let them know we trust them, we trust their work, and accept that this one mistake is one mistake."

The inspector arrived at 0956, she was waiting in the main lobby. Her dark brown hair tied into a donut bun. Black pantsuit, brown undershirt, brown loafers, brown glasses, and carried a dark brown leather satchel.

She reached out her hand, "My name is Eva."

"I apologize, since Covid, I've learned I don't enjoy shaking hands. I'm Liam, Director of Transfusion Medicine. Do you mind if we take the stairs? The lab is one floor above us?"

Eva agreed. On the second floor, one side of the hallway was glass, the cafeteria and main entrance visible below. Framed posters of the CEO, COO, and CNO lined the off white wall on the other side of the hall. The C-suite members sat at individual AI generated Thanksgiving tables. Holiday platitudes disguised as bad puns captioned their photos.

"Grateful for all you do at Drivers."

"At Drivers, we're all Family."

"Let us be Thankful for Drivers."

The lab's empty office served as a welcome room. "We can microwave the coffee if it's not warm enough." Stacked next to the Malaky's Coffee travel box were emerald green paper cups with their trademark white cat perched on a broom. "We thought you'd be here a couple of hours ago. The donuts should still be fresh."

"No. I don't eat any food prepared or presented by any lab." She opened a notebook, "Were you suggesting I'm late?"

"Not at all. I apologize. My supervisor said you would be here first thing. I assumed that meant 0730. In all honesty, I want to thank you. I canceled three meetings anticipating your arrival. This has been my most productive morning in months. I know we're about to get started, but that bag of yours is nice." Liam held out his hand then recoiled from touching it. "May I ask where you got it?"

"You may not. If you're ready, I'd like to begin the survey now."

Second Observation: "Firm members not readily cooperative. Example: Techs gawked upon inspector and attempted to evade interaction with inspector."

Liam offered Eva a tour of the lab, but she declined. She spent the first thirty minutes walking around in silence, Liam following. Occasionally, a tech would make eye contact with her. If they smiled, she would nod in return. If they did nothing but stare or turn away, she made a note.

No one in the lab spoke. Liam couldn't tell if the lack of chatter was normal for first shift or if they were trying to stay below Eva's radar.

Phones were answered on the first ring. Computers displayed the LIS. Everyone appeared busy. Everyone except Quinneth. Quinneth held her phone under the lab bench like was still in high school.

Eva took out a bottle of sanitizer from her bag and cleaned her hands before offering her right. "Hi, I'm Eva, you are?"

"Quinneth," she said, sliding her phone beneath her thigh. The tips of her fingers tapped Eva's hand.

"Would you mind showing me your irradiation process?" Eva didn't smile, but she wasn't harsh.

"Oh, uhm, I'm in automated today."

Liam drew in a deep breath.

"That's okay," Eva said. "This will only take a few minutes."

"I'll have Malia cover your bench while you're with the inspector," Liam said. He wasn't going to let Quinneth respond with another stupid excuse.

Third observation: "Ensure techs are familiar with procedures prior to signing off as competent."

"Go ahead and irradiate any product." Eva held her notebook at the ready.

Quinneth's eyes met Liam's. They were begging for help. "Os are always good," he said. *Get out of your chair.*

She fumbled over choosing a unit until the door ajar alarm sounded. "Any unit is okay," said Liam. No longer hiding the annoyance. *She embarrassed me in front of Dr. Sanders yesterday. Today, she's acting like she's never followed verbal instructions.*

"We only have As and AB." Quinneth held one of each type in her hands.

"Is it common for this lab to irradiate thawed plasma?" Eva asked.

Liam shook his head behind the inspector's back.

"Uhm, no?" Quinneth squeezed the units of plasma. "I thought that's what you asked me to irradiate."

"Sorry for the confusion," Eva smiled over her shoulder. "I did state any product. I would prefer a unit of packed red blood cells."

Bag of O positive in hand, Quinneth walked at glacial speed to the irradiator. Her hands shook as she tried to attach the irradiation indicator sticker. "Oh, I forgot to write the date and my initials," she said to Eva.

"You haven't put it in the irradiator. You still have time. I understand I make techs nervous. How long have you worked here?"

"I started in August." Quinneth scribbled in red ink. She managed to log into the irradiator and press start without any additional fumbles.

"So you missed the freight fest. Probably better for everyone you weren't here." Notebook at the ready, Eva asked, "Can you tell me how you know the irradiation process is complete?"

"Yes, the machine beeps."

Is she smiling? Does she think that's an acceptable answer?

Liam forced a laugh, "Nice to know you can keep a sense of humor while you're nervous. Please explain the three things we look for after the machine beeps."

Last night, he didn't care if they passed. This morning, Dr. Sanders pointed out this would be Liam's first inspection as manager. The old manager never failed. He knew Dr. Sanders was manipulating him into caring. He was annoyed it worked.

Quinneth pressed her lips together then pulled a notebook out of her pocket. She flipped through several pages. "Bars full." She tapped a power icon on the machine. "Count display is one hundred. Sticker is blacked out."

Liam held a poker face. He emailed the lab a month ago reminding new techs that handwritten notes were not allowed at the bench. They should follow all procedures as written or ask for help if they do not understand.

Fourth observation: "Firm has continued problems with irradiation documentation."

The irradiator beeped. Quinneth removed the unit from the drawer and handed it to Eva.

"Is this part of your process?" Eva asked, not accepting the unit.

Quinneth stood, arm out, staring at Liam for guidance.

"If it passed a visual inspection, go ahead and do the LIS portion of the process," Liam spoke slow and soft to conceal his rage.

"Sorry, you just said irradiate. LIS means the computer part, right?"

After three attempts, the new label printed, and she verified it in the LIS.

"Thank you so much, Quinneth," Eva smiled.

Standing in silence as Quinneth perfectly recreated the error that brought the FDA to Drivers, Liam had one thought. Two thoughts. *I could kill her. I could kill her and no one would know.*

A shadow crossed Liam's face, taking his gaze away from the rest of the report.

"How'd we do?" Dr. Sanders took his usual chair and fished out a piece of hard candy.

"We passed. Only one observation was a serious offense. We have several minor corrections to document."

Liam prepared for the inevitable speech from Dr. Sanders. He wanted to triage irradiated orders months ago. Liam fought back. First, it was one more phone call to make before issuing products. Second, the purpose of triages is to prevent patient harm. Giving irradiated blood is safe for everyone. Sure, the red cells are less viable, but only if it was a fresh unit to begin with. Lastly, he was tired of Drivers making his techs, therefore himself, responsible for things providers should be doing.

"Liam." Ryker opened his door without knocking.

"I'm assuming this is important." He glared.

She made awkward motions with her hands, like she was literally trying to pick words out of the air, "Do...you...know..."

"Ryker, I'm in a meeting."

"If someone's already dead, do we call 911 or the non-emergency line?"

Dr. Sanders unwrapped another candy.

"I don't know." *What a strange question.* "Can I get back to you on that?" *She couldn't be serious?.*

"That's okay," she said.

Liam exchanged glances with Dr. Sanders.

Ryker's voice traveled from the open door of the tissue coordinator's office, "This is Ryker in transfusion. I found an unalive person on campus. Is this the appropriate number?"

Chapter 2

Current Day

THE CONFERENCE ROOM WAS the same one she'd been in dozens of times. The tables were arranged in a rectangular semicircle, like she was going to watch a presentation on the pull-down screen. With her luck, they probably had a PowerPoint handy for such occasions. "The Do's and Don'ts of Killing Your Coworkers."

At this point, Ryker couldn't tell if the room was freezing or if she was having a trauma response. The door opens to a familiar face.

"Ryker Graden, we've got to stop meeting like this," Felice Harris says as she enters the room. "I heard you disagreed with our method of detainment." She sits in the first available chair. The previous lab manager used to sit there while reading staff meeting slides word for word from the screen.

"This is a weird way to offer me a job." They handcuffed Ryker to the chair dead center, despite her protests. Not because she didn't deserve it. Being handcuffed to a rolling chair is fucking stupid. Albeit, an escape wouldn't be easy, or fast, but still. To prove her point, Ryker pushed the chair away from the table, settling against the wall. "If I wanted to, I could probably get out of this," she says.

"Then I guess you must like it." Felice deadpans.

"I guess you must like it," Ryker repeats, mocking her captor.

Without standing, Felice rolls her chair back and knocks on the door behind her. "Will you correct this?" she asks into the void of the cracked-open door.

A guy wearing black scrubs enters and unlocks the cuffs around the chair. Felice points to the table. Ryker obeys, scooting herself back to her original placement.

"Good girl."

Hiding facial expressions is not a skill Ryker possesses. If she had to guess, Felice saw all levels of confusion, anger, and amusement.

"I want you to explain everything that happened tonight."

"What time do you want me to start?" Ryker yawns, loud and proud.

"Now, unless you want the handcuffs back on." Felice raises her hand as if to knock on the door again.

"No. You said *tonight*. It's what, 0100? You want starting at 0001, that's boring. Or do you mean tonight as in, yesterday?" Having spent seven years on night shift, Ryker knew clarification was key. Yesterday and today can be a matter of sleep and wake cycles or they can have a strict midnight separation.

"I want you to tell me everything that happened."

"Got it. It was a butt load. We're talking British Bake Off tiered cakes in Wranglers, and I'm pretty tired, so I might..."

"You will begin your account with your next sentence."

"Yes, ma'am...Shit."

Monday: Ten Days Ago

USUALLY BY NOVEMBER, THE fresh crop of residents had tightened their game. Not this guy.

"Transfusion, this is Ryker, how may I help you?"

"Yes, hello, this is the transfusion services resident. I'm calling to order a STAT Red Blood Cell Exchange."

He always forgets to include his name when he's identifying himself.

"Is this a new order, and can you give me the patient's medical record number?"

"Yes, I'm placing the order now."

That's what she gets for asking Dr. Kudela a two-part question.

"Did you place the order in SAGA, and can I have the MRN?" Ryker moved her cursor to the Drivers LIS. Five years ago, Drivers upgraded their LIS to an all-encompassing system. Which did not encompass blood banking. The blood bank, probably other departments, had to find a different operating system. One that was compatible with SAGA.

"I thought because it was STAT, I could do a verbal order."

The fucking audacity.

"I am only allowed to issue uncrossmatched blood via a verbal order. Is this exchange uncrossmatched?" Throwing out the "u" word made most uncooperative providers listen the hell up.

"No. No. I was confused. I will put in the order now, thanks." He hung up without giving her the MRN.

I guess that's my fault for not asking a third time.

Working desk would be an easy shift, if it weren't for all the human interaction. Answering the same question for eight hours, "Yes that blood is ready." And making the same phone calls for eight hours, "You need to write your ID number on your request form. Can I please have your tube station? Blood is ready for patient XXX." A bad night on desk is more draining than any other bench assignment. These last few months, not having a consistent backup made those nights happen more often.

Ryker sent a Teams message to Yvette, "Dr. Kudela tried to phone in a STAT RBCX. I asked him to place an order. He wouldn't give me the MRN."

After the outbreak, they filled leadership positions as soon as possible. Malia tossed her hat into the ring for second shift supervisor. Malia's title had the word senior, but Yvette had more experience. Liam made the right choice.

"Transfusion, this is Ryker...The order has not printed...Can I have the MRN...We already have an exchange crossmatched for this patient. First shift got it ready this afternoon...Dr. Sanders put in the order...I was told it was ready, I assumed that meant they paged apheresis...It has not been picked up...Yes, I will let her know right now...Thanks."

Therapeutic apheresis, or red blood cell exchanges, can be prophylactic or emergent. Using an apheresis machine, the patient's malformed red blood cells are removed and replaced with healthy, fresh donor red blood cells. Prophylactic exchanges occur every four to six weeks. On occasion, due to some triggering event, a patient comes to the Emergency Room in sickle cell crisis. Emergency exchanges are time-sensitive and occur after the onset of crisis symptoms.

This patient arrived with a trauma alias. Drivers treats too many trauma patients in one day to use John or Jane Doe. The emergency department opted for a system based on the NATO phonetic alphabet.

In the blood bank LIS, a sickle cell diagnosis prompts special comments to be added to the patient's chart. "Delta, B," had none listed. Just the basics. Blood type, O negative. Antibody screen, negative.

No antibodies is a plus.

Before adding the requirements herself, Ryker wanted to verify this was indeed a person with sickle cell disease, and she wasn't given the wrong MRN. A few weeks ago, this same resident ordered a STAT Red Blood Cell Exchange for someone who didn't have sickle cell disease. Didn't even have sickle cell trait. The patient was desperate for pain meds and was willing to trade their blood to ease their burden. Prior to issuing the red cells, Yvette checked their complete blood count. Hemoglobin measured 14.6.

Tonight, the GEN lab performed a hemoglobin electrophoresis soon after the patient was admitted. Hemoglobin S measured eighty-seven percent, a positive result for sickle cell anemia. The manual differential featured a classic presentation of sickle cell anemia. Target cells, polychromasia, sickle cells, basophilic stippling, and retics. *Stomatocytes are different. Blue-green neutrophilic inclusions? Interesting.*

"Hemoglobin 4.6. That adds up. RDW 24? Did they get blood somewhere else?" Trauma patient, no external data. A few clicks of the LIS revealed the ABORh testing was performed in tubes. "Why did we do that?" Ryker often spoke out loud to the LIS. Between the constant flow of her internal monologue and the extraneous noises from the lab, talking out loud helped her focus.

Coupled with the new employees, the contract Drivers had with the solid phase instrumentation expired. Liam wanted to wait until the blood bank was fully staffed before installing the new gel analyzers. Admin decided it was a great opportunity to train the new employees alongside the current employees. Meaning, Drivers would not pay to extend the contract on the old machines. Admin left it to Liam to figure out the details.

The old instrumentation had a strict workflow. Deviations from that workflow were investigated, interrogated, and interdicted. Old machines with previous employees. Now, the old rules were out the window. The new workflow was "to be determined" after implantation. With half of the staff in training, and the other half focusing on their own convenience, the wild west of blood banking began.

Thoroughness is both a blessing and a curse. Ryker could have minded her own business. She could have accepted first shift completed the exchange according to their policies. She wanted to believe in the accuracy of first shift, but her gut couldn't.

SAGA, the hospital's electronic health record, had a flag in the upper left corner, "Patient marked for merge." This happens when a patient has been registered under multiple medical record numbers, and they need to combine the information. With no alias listed, she scrolled the chart notes.

"Patient name: Desmund Nwadike. Patient found by sister, in home, unconscious. Sister called 911. Patient brought to Drivers under trauma MRN. See MRN XXXXXX for history."

Ryker recognized the name from their sickle cell program. As expected, the alternate MRN pulled up a full chart in the blood bank LIS. No previous antibodies. Requires blood negative for C, E, and K antigens, easy enough. Blood type O positive. *What the fuck?*

Under the trauma MRN, the patient typed as O negative. *How did we mess that up?*

The answer was Quinneth. A new hire who was fast-tracked, like Elyssa, but somehow lacked the quintessential med tech skill of critical thinking.

It's possible with regular transfusions of O negative blood, the patient's own D antigen was diluted, and testing appeared negative. Before investigating further, Ryker messaged Yvette, "STAT RBCX, we typed them as O neg today. We have a history of O pos and another MRN, I'm paging Sandman now."

Sandman, a nickname she would never say to his face, was their medical director. Dr. Sanders called within a minute of being paged.

"Transfusion, this is Ryker...Yes, Dr. Sanders, it's about the STAT exchange patient...I understand your email saying we can waive antigen requirements for STAT exchanges. I wasn't here when they got the units ready...I was told they were waiting for apheresis to come pick it up...I'm the one who paged Regina...I have a different question...We typed the patient as O negative today. He has an alternate MRN, historically, he is O positive...No, they haven't merged the charts yet...Weak D testing, sure...Thanks."

An alarm from the tube station indicated it was full. Ryker hoped it was being dramatic, and one or two tubes formed the perfect stack to activate the sensor. *Shit.* Full. Engrossed by the RBCX mystery, Ryker tuned out the six carriers that fell into her care.

The alarm also got the attention of Elyssa, who came up from her spot in manual to help empty the tube station. Two requests for blood products, three pink tops for automated, and a set of blood cultures that Ryker immediately sent to the GEN LAB microbiology department.

"Thanks, I'll get all this. Can you start weak D testing Delta, B, the exchange patient?"

Elyssa removed the pink tops from their biohazard bags and matched them to their orders. Ryker felt Elyssa's eyes peering over her shoulder. "I thought we typed them O neg?" she asked.

"Someone did. Hence, the weak D. Dr. Sanders said he knows the patient, but we can't give blood based on personal knowledge. Issuing all O negative units would be a major misuse of inventory."

"TLDR, first shift fucked up." Elyssa rolled her eyes.

Ryker paused, uncertain of what to make of the beginning of Elyssa's sentence. The end was accurate, so she moved on. "Quinneth specifically. I'm sure she had help."

Order of importance, issue blood products first. Instead of printing the actual request form, someone chose a sheet of hieroglyphs. Zero patient identifiers, nothing indicating what product they wanted, and no phone number.

She could put the form in the shred bin and wait for an irate nurse to call but Ryker was not in the mood to get yelled at tonight. One of the random series of fonts appeared to be a product unit number. Reverse engineering the problem, she looked up the unit in the blood bank LIS to find the MRN of the patient. She typed that MRN into SAGA, found the patient's current care team, and called the number listed under primary nurse.

"Yeah." A hint of attitude in his voice that made Ryker immediately regret her decision to be helpful.

Uhhg. Be nice. Be nice.

"This is Ryker in transfusion. Did you send a request for blood products for patient Anwar in room 136?"

"Yeah."

Be nice. Be nice.

"So, the form you sent me isn't the correct request form. You need to send either the transfusion order or the product order."

"What did I send you?" he asked.

Fuck if I know.

"Honestly, I'm not sure what exact document you printed, but it is not either of the forms I mentioned."

"Can't you just use that one?"

"No. This form doesn't have any patient information on it, it doesn't list the ordering provider, it doesn't even tell me what product you want."

"I want blood."

Omg. Omg.

"I will send that to you as soon as I get the correct request form."

"I sent you the form."

Ryker took a deep breath and clenched the heart stress ball in her labcoat pocket. "Like I said, I don't know what form this is, it doesn't have any patient infor..."

"If it doesn't have any patient information on it, how did you know who it was for?" His voice smug, like he caught Ryker in a lie.

"I figured it out because I'm good at my job. I'm trying to do what's best for the patient. I cannot issue blood based on the form you sent me. Please print and send one of the two forms, the transfuse order or the product order, and I will issue the blood."

Muffled chatter in the background.

"This is Cecilia, ICU charge. This patient needs blood STAT. My nurse is telling me you won't send it."

"Hi, Cecilia, this is Ryker in transfusion. That statement your nurse made is not quite accurate. I said I will send the blood as soon as I get the correct request form."

"I saw him put the form in the tube station."

"I have *a* form. It might be a screenshot of a unit transfused earlier today. It doesn't have any of the information I need. As soon as I get the correct form, I will issue blood."

"Show me what you printed?" Cecilia asked, obviously not a question for Ryker. "No. I told you it's not the first screen. You have to click the message at the bottom, then print the screen that pops up." Then to Ryker, "Sorry about that. He's sending the correct form now."

"Thanks. Hey, will you ask him to put his employee ID and tube station on the form?"

"He didn't do that either?" she asked with the icy chill of a charge nurse who's had enough of someone's shit for the night. "Are you still wearing that? I told you it's against Drivers policy. You weren't even here."

As far as Ryker knew, her space cat and pizza slices lanyard met safety guidelines. The breakaway snap was so loose it fell off while standing. It happened in front of Liam once. Her badge landed on the floor between her feet. Felt like her bra snapped and her boobs popped out of her labcoat.

Then Cecilia said, "We will send the correct form. Thank you."

"Thanks." Ryker hung up the phone and applauded the universe for the immediate justice. She checked the printer for any sneaky uncrossmatched or massive transfusion orders. None lay in the pile. She received the waiting samples before checking in with Elyssa and the weak D testing.

Weak D blood antigens have similar performance issues as some men. It requires a lot of heat and incubation to get them to a full expression.

The D antigens on the surface of the red blood cells are depressed, giving weak or sometimes no reaction at the immediate spin phase of testing. Weak D testing consists of allowing the patient's red blood cells to incubate at 37 degrees with anti-D antisera and then spinning and reading the tube.

If the reaction is still too weak or negative, testing continues. Wash the red cells four times. Add anti-human antiglobulin (Anti-IgG) antisera to a dry cell button. Spin and read the tube. Samples still weak or negative after this phase are considered D, or Rh negative.

Samples with a strong reaction after either 37 degrees or Anti-IgG are considered D or Rh positive.

In the instance of a patient whose Rh positive blood has been replaced with majority Rh negative blood, the weak D testing could enhance the small percentage of sample that is natural to the patient. Making it more visible during testing. It would not make the Rh negative donor blood test positive.

"I see a two plus with mixed field." Yvette documented her reactions on a downtime reporting sheet. "This doesn't even need weak D testing. The mixed field is justified by the exchange two months ago."

A mixed field reaction occurs when there are multiple cell populations in a sample. This is a warning sign that the patient has been transfused within ninety days. Because you are testing both the patient's blood and the donor blood circulating in their body, you get two different reactions in the same tube. Agglutination for a positive reaction, and a cloud dissipating off the agglutination for the negative cell population. Without a blood history, it is not acceptable to assume which one is the patient's blood type.

"I saw the same thing. That's why I wanted you to look at it." Elyssa handed Yvette her results.

There's no way.

"June, can you see if they ran the sample on the instrument?" Ryker asked.

There, captured in full color, a textbook mixed field in gel. Strong agglutination at the top of the well, and a button on the bottom. Bright red x's covered the test result.

"She rejected it and did tube testing." June gave Yvette the print-out.

"I don't understand how she missed it." Elyssa shook her head.

"No time to figure out how. I'll update Dr. Sanders and the patient's blood type in the LIS. Ryker, what's our O neg inventory? Call ABI and see if they can replace the units first shift crossmatched. If not, we'll switch to O pos. I don't know if Regina can wait for us to antigen test more units."

"The email from Dr. Sanders said..."

"I know what it says." Yvette interrupted. "Fatima had them set up C, E, and K negative units, I want to verify that we can waive those requirements." Yvette left the sample and took the worksheets to her office.

As a tech, Yvette wouldn't have second-guessed following the previous guidance. Ryker couldn't tell if Yvette was mad at her, annoyed by her, insecure with their new dynamic, or all of the above. The more practical answer, Ryker needed to stop projecting. Let Yvette handle her business.

"We have forty-two O negs, including the ones for the RBCX. ABI was going to send us three tonight, they cannot send more." Ryker messaged Yvette.

Dr. Kudela's number appeared on the caller ID.

"Transfusion, this is Ryker...We never got your order...Yvette is talking to him now...You don't have the authority the waive the antigen requirements...All deviations require medical director level approval...We are going as fast as we can...Thanks."

"Transfusion, this is Ryker...Hey Regina, we're still working on it...We're hoping we can switch to O pos units...We wouldn't have enough for traumas if we used the O negs...I can tell you how, but it won't make you feel any better...I'll page you when it's ready."

Twenty minutes later, Regina was at the blood bank window with her apheresis machine. Dr. Sanders waived the antigen requirements. Sulfur from the sickle cell testing buffer lingered in the air.

"Do you know what the volume is?" Regina asked as Ryker scanned the units for issuing.

"Total is 2960 milliliters."

"Where's the purple stickers?"

"What?" Ryker heard what Regina asked, she wasn't anticipating that question. It threw her out of context.

"The ER thinks he might have leukemia." Regina was the charge nurse for the apheresis team. She was also one of the longest-term employees at Drivers. She had the shortest digit employee id number still in use.

It wasn't that Ryker didn't believe Regina. Plenty of times, Regina knew more about her patient's condition than the blood bank residents. Thoroughness got her into this mess, it was the only way out. Still unable to locate the original paper order, Ryker reopened the electronic version in SAGA. Instead of selecting "irradiated" from the special requirement drop-down menu, they selected "none." Underneath "none," the provider typed, "Dear Blood Bank, please type and cross irradiated units. AML possible cause of crisis."

Fuck.

One more step before the units could be issued. Well three. They would need to be returned as crossmatched, irradiated, then re-issued. Less than four minutes to for each irradiation cycle. Three units max per cycle. It was another twenty minutes until Regina left with the exchange.

We're definitely going to hear about this tomorrow.

Ryker stacked the crossmatch tag slips from the exchange and reached for the automatic stapler. Nothing happened. She sighed, taking the manual stapler off the back counter. Click, nothing. The drawer at desk used to store backup supplies was completely empty.

I really hate first shift.

Chapter 3

FROM A STEP STOOL in the back of a small crowd, Sunny bobbed her head back and forth to keep a clear view. A man in a green bejeweled robe entered the room. The audience, all in white coats, awed at his presence. Some bowed their heads.

This was her first assignment with the agency. A two-hundred-bed hospital in rural Oklahoma. The agency didn't give her instructions. Didn't give any hint as to what she was supposed to look out for or report. One month in, and she could feel the vibes were off, but she didn't get any sense the source was supernatural. If anything, it felt like a cult. At least, what she thought a cult would feel like. She never officially joined one.

No one cussed in the lab. No one. During training, she thawed the wrong control for their brand new chemistry analyzer. She didn't notice until she put it on the instrument and the pop-up message to refill the control didn't go away. "Son of a bitch," she whispered to herself. Horror crossed her trainer's face. "Oh, sorry, it slipped out."

"I feel the words that slip out tend to be the ones we use most often." Her trainer, Judith, stared with harsh judgment. Sunny turned to the chemistry analyzer, wrote down the control she needed on the back of her gloved hand, and walked to the freezers for a second time.

The man in green carried a large black medieval book and a shiny gold mace with a leather handle. His height loomed over the crowd of willing and less-willing participants. Sunny shivered with anticipation.

She'd worked at places where they pretended cussing wasn't allowed. Her old lab director brought it up during a few staff meetings, but no one took it seriously. Here, it wasn't just curse words. It was anything that could be construed as "negative." During her second of three new hire reviews, Sunny was told that her coworkers found her to be *prickly*. No one had ever called her that. She was a god damn ball of sunshine, it's in her name.

"The way you react to phone calls from nurses is the example most people give," Judith explained.

"I'm always nice on the phone." Sunny frowned, unable to make sense of the cactus comparison.

"When you get off the phone? You made fun of a nurse for you to add on a basic metabolic panel to a PT."

"She demanded I change out the lids to make the blue top a green top."

"Yes, we all heard you say that. I don't know how things worked at your other hospitals, but we respect our nurses. Their job is stressful. It's our job to accommodate their stress."

"You can't add that test to that sample. The potassium would be off the charts, not to mention the other values."

"I'm not saying you should have done what she requested, but you could have shown more empathy."

"What about empathy for me, or the lab? She yelled at me for like three minutes."

"She relieved a bit of stress over the phone."

"And I relieved my stress when I hung up."

"That's why your coworkers find you prickly. They never know what you will say behind their backs."

Sunny spent her lunch break crying in the bathroom that day. Tears continued for most of the night. The next morning, she resolved to destroy whatever hidden dangers lurked in the shadows of that hospital.

Today, on this stool, she felt it in her bones. They were in danger. This couldn't be right. The air was tight. It stretched between those yearning to be in this room and the others who wanted to flee. Their feet frozen by their sympathetic nervous system. Her heart beat so hard her jaw twitched.

The tall man chanted something. His voice rang out much too loud for the number of people huddled in the corner before him.

Everyone chanted back. Everyone except Sunny. She didn't know there was audience participation.

The tall man spotted her.

He knows. He knows I'm with the agency.

Judith invited her. Claimed it was *optional*. Ryker warned Sunny about mandatory fun days.

As the man locked his eyes on her, Sunny held her breath.

Why am I standing on a stupid stool? Good for viewing. Bad for fighting. Was surviving the outbreak at Drivers a fluke? Did she become arrogant? How stupid could she be? At the very least, she should have checked in with Felice, told her where she was going. This is her first case, she didn't want the SSB to think couldn't hack it. There was definitely something wrong at this hospital. It was coming straight for her with a gorgeous mace.

"Ahhh," Sunny screamed and fell off the stool. She held her arms in front of her face, waiting for the blow. She screamed again when something hit her arm. It didn't hurt. It was...wet? More droplets sprinkled over her face and exposed hands. She opened her eyes. The man waved his mace over the crowd. Judith was on her knees, kissing a rosemary.

The priest chanted more, walking around the lab, adorning the new chemistry analyzers with the oil in his aspergillum. When he returned to the lab employees, he made the sign of the cross and said, "May the almighty God bless you. The father, the son, and the holy spirit."

"Amen," replied the group, minus Sunny, who was picking herself up from the floor.

Chapter 4

Current Day

"So the exchange patient, Desmund Nwadike, he was the first victim?" Felice asks. No paper. No pen. No apparent recording device.

"Oh, I have no idea who the *first* victim was." Ryker swipes at a patch of dry skin on her lips. "Can I get some warm water?"

"Why did I listen to ten minutes about an RBC exchange?"

"Because," Ryker pulls her ear lobe, "Fatima told me it was taken care of, and it wasn't."

"That is a conversation for your therapist. Tell me something important and I'll get you...tepid water?"

"First off, this is a judgment-free space."

"It is not."

"Secondly, if it weren't for that exchange, none of this," Ryker wafted her hands in the air, "Would have happened. And yes, he was *a* victim, but I didn't know that yet. Third, warm water is a very normal drink. I'd prefer it with a splash of lemon, but I didn't want to come across as needy. Lastly, and thank you for reminding me, my therapist quit."

"Get to the murders."

Tuesday: Nine Days Ago

RYKER WAITED AT THE employee elevators. How many more days of her life could she give to this job? How many times had she waited for the elevator, feeling like she just walked out of it? As if home were a fairy tale place, and this hell was the only reality. Stupid stress dreams. Waking up throughout the night because no one unloaded the centrifuge is annoying as fuck. First, you tell yourself you don't have a centrifuge at home, you can't unload it. The second time you wake up, you scold yourself. You're not at work. The third time, you gasp and sit straight up in bed. It's more exhausting than dreaming about a giant goat-man chasing you through the woods. You want to run, but your legs won't move as fast as they should.

Four minutes since she pressed the button. Two minutes left to clock in. She'd lost this game before. According to Liam, "Everyone takes the same elevators. It's not like they slow them down for second shift."

Patient transport elevators stood at the ready in the opposite corner of the hall. She hated using them. It was against the rules. A rule Ryker respected. What if a patient was waiting when she got off? Those elevators were so much faster. She pushed the button for the second floor. The race was on. Which elevator, employee or transport, would pick her up first?

To her surprise, the employee elevator chimed its welcome. As the doors opened, Ryker's frustration grew. She wasn't mad at the employee. She wasn't mad they had to remove giant food tray carts from the elevator. Everyone has their job. She was mad at the elevator system for setting her up to fail. Mad at Liam for not believing this happened every day. Really, she was mad at herself for letting four minutes determine the tone of her day. She shouldn't have folded her scrubs. She shouldn't have stared at her phone for so long. If she hadn't had that third beer last night, she would have woken up at her first alarm.

Speaking of, the elevator alarm sounded. The guy, unbothered by noise, pushed and adjusted a second heavy cart. He struggled steering it out the door without hitting the first. The transport elevator chimed, the lift was empty. One minute left.

A gaggle of suits took up an inconsiderate amount of space on the second-floor hallway. Head down, she sifted through, avoiding all eye contact. Not that she'd heard of anyone getting in trouble for using the transport elevators, but still. The target on her back grew daily. The entire lab watched her, waiting for her to screw up.

Seven minutes after the hour. Right on time. Folded clothes for the rest of the week, relaxing revenge procrastination, and three more beers in the fridge. No lessons learned today.

"There she is, that's everyone."

Liam announcing someone's arrival was never a good sign. Two suits migrated from the elevators to the specimen processing bench. The lab techs stood in a semicircle across from them. Ryker took a spot on the edge, next to Quinneth. It wasn't her first choice, but it was the fastest way to stop moving and redirect attention away from herself. Quinneth shifted a step away.

"This is a brief safety huddle." Dr. Sanders, tall, slender, sixtyish years old. Notorious polka dot bow tie prominent under his chin. His tapered pants hemmed two inches shy of his dress shoes, showing off the matching polka dot socks.

"Hello all, I want to introduce you to our current resident, Dr. Kudela." He motioned with his hand and continued. "We had an issue with a sickle cell exchange yesterday. There was some confusion on both the lab's and the resident's part regarding how we proceed with STAT exchanges. The patient will most likely die soon."

The crowd gasped.

"My apologies, I did not intend for it to be that dramatic. Their prognosis is not due to anything any of you did. There was the obvious issue of the mistyping. Fatima will address that with a guide for when the instruments flag a mixed field. The other issue was timing. Had you adhered to my previous instructions," he gave Fatima a hard stare, "The O neg units would have been out the door by the afternoon. There was a failure to communicate with the apheresis team."

Fucking finally. First shift and Fatima are being put in their places. You can't just make up your own policies. You can't ignore patient results because they are confusing.

"The main reason I'm talking to you today."

Now for the thank you to second shift for fixing their bullshit.

"The exchange requested irradiation. Somehow, Liam can explain the technical issues, we gave out a unit that was irradiated physically, but not in the LIS. It was transfused during the exchange last night. This morning, we reported it to the FDA."

Ryker met eyes with Liam, he nodded. *God dammit.*

"Symptomatically, they were concerned about leukemia-induced lactic acidosis. We will monitor the patient's labs for the duration of their admission and circle back with the FDA on whether or not irradiation was indicated. That being said, I've noticed providers adding the irradiation requirement more frequently to patients who, frankly, don't need it. Our normal process was to have a supervisor go through the red cell orders of the previous day. New irradiation requests would be reported to myself and the residents. We would discuss and remove any requirement we deemed not indicated." He stood with Liam on his right and Dr. Kudela, a younger guy in an ill-fitting suit on his left.

It was difficult to listen while simultaneously cursing herself out. Luckily, Ryker had plenty of practice. She scanned the crowd to project her judgments elsewhere. This was a shame-inducing departmental failure. Yet most of her coworkers kept glancing at the clock.

"Part of reporting incidents to the FDA is offering a solution. We've tried making techs circle or highlight the requirement. We've tried making the requirements print in a different color, so the highlighting was done for you. Now we're doing something new. It will be more work for all of us, but hopefully it will prevent us from having to report technicalities to the FDA."

Ryker covered her mouth as she fought back a yawn.

"Are we boring you?" Dr. Kudela glared.

With all eyes on Ryker, again, she guessed he was talking to her. "No," she said.

"Ryker is one of our second shift techs," Dr. Sanders explained. "This is her seven am. I've seen Ryker yawn while running two MTPs."

That was nice. Weird. Why does Dr. Sanders know who I am? I know who he is. We've met before. Still.

"Starting today," Dr. Sanders continued. "All orders with new irradiation requirements will be triaged through my resident. Dr. Kudela will approve or disapprove the requirement prior to you issuing products."

Of course, Ryker had questions. "What if the order is for the operating room or labor and delivery?" Something in her periphery caught her attention. *Did Kudela make a face at me?*

"Good question. Yawn forgiven." Dr. Sanders hoisted himself onto the counter. His muted plaid slacks in direct contact with laboratory contaminants. "If the order is for a floor we do not currently triage products, we will not triage the irradiation. Although, how often do you see that as newly added to OR orders?"

"Fair." *There it is again.* Ryker kept an eye on Dr. Kudela. "You're right, it isn't common. The last time we adjusted our triage guidelines, we didn't make any exceptions. Labor and delivery almost climbed through the window. I thought that nurse was going to rip my head off and collect the blood volcano-ing from my neck." Ryker knew she was talking too much. She should have ended after her first sentence. The longer she spoke, the further out of his mouth Dr. Kudela shoved his tongue. Not straight out like a child. Sideways. Sideways. She kept speaking because she couldn't believe it.

"Thank you for that reminder and the delectable imagery. So, like I said, not for OR or L and D," Dr. Sanders said.

Dr. Kudela's tongue went back inside.

"What about patients whose diagnosis matches our policy for irradiated blood?" Ryker knew she was the annoying person who kept meetings long. But she wanted clarity, and wanted it directly from the source.

"For now, let's triage those."

"Even for neonates?"

Dr. Kudela's tongue shot out sideways.

Is no one else seeing this?

"Our newborn protocol policy has us add the irradiation requirement as soon as we test the baby's sample. Are we going to change this part of our policy?" she asked.

"You are correct. I spoke too quickly." Again, Dr. Sander's voice reeled in Dr. Kudela's tongue. "I'm not interested in neonates. We will not change that process. Any other questions?" Dr. Sanders hopped down, indicating he was ready to leave. The teal socks with yellow polka dots still visible.

To everyone's surprise, Quinneth raised her hand. "What about for a massive transfusion?"

An awkward silence descended.

"Don't we have a policy that addresses this?" Dr. Sanders faced Liam directly.

"Yes, we do. I will continue this discussion with the lab and let you know if there is anything else we need from you."

Ryker couldn't tell if Liam was embarrassed or shocked by the question.

Liam paused until the door closed behind Dr. Sanders and Dr. Kudela. "During an MTP, all requirements are waived. That includes antibodies, freshness, sickle cell testing, and irradiation. That has been and will continue to be our practice. Any other questions?"

For the third time in less than an hour, Ryker felt the eyes of a crowd on her. She shook her head.

"Thank you to first shift for staying. I also want to remind everyone about the Thanksgiving Hero and Memorial Dinner next Tuesday. There will be a brief presentation, one free meal, a drink, and choice of pie for dessert. Will Ryker and Elyssa come with me to my office?"

First shift darted for the door.

"Who's going to work with me?" June asked. "I can't run the lab by myself."

"I'm here," Yvette raised her hand. "I just need to grab my labcoat."

Chapter 5

Tuesday: Nine Days Ago

"**My sister is a** med tech, she and Ryker have similar communication styles." Dr. Kudela struggled to match stride with Dr. Sanders.

"Asking questions is different than questioning your authority. You have to learn not to assume it's a personal attack."

"Did I do the tongue thing?" Dr. Kudela grimaced.

"You did. You know, as rude as people think Ryker is, I know she saw it. Maybe cut her some slack for not pointing it out to the entire department. Despite the rumors from the outbreak, she technically hasn't murdered anyone."

The walk to the STAT lab left Dr. Kudela short of breath. He didn't enjoy Ryker's threat of uncrossmatched blood. Or Dr. Sanders laughing when he told him about it last night. This meeting was going to be his show of strength. Instead, he got so uncomfortable standing in front of all those people he revealed his nervous tick. Then again, his sister always beat him in arguments, too. He thought things would be different after he became a doctor. Thought the white coat would come with a boost of confidence. He had big plans at Drivers. He needed to find the nerve to follow through.

"Andy, I wanted to introduce Dr. Kudela in person. He's the one who made you go through all those logbooks. That new crystal sickle cell case would make for an excellent addition to his study." The STAT lab buzzed with instrumentation. It wasn't Dr. Kudlea's first time in the lab, but he had not been in it enough to have the layout memorized. "Dr. Kudela, Andy here is our senior hematology tech. He's our first line of defense against false reporting on blood smears. You're in good hands." Dr. Sanders took his leave.

"Hi, Dr. Kudela. I was just printing the latest record you requested. Do you mind my asking what got you so interested in the crystals?"

"My mom. She died, suddenly, when I was young."

"Oh," Andy said, "I'm so sorry."

"It's okay, I'm used to telling the story. My older sister and I never got the answers we wanted about what happened. We both found our way into healthcare majors. Once we had some insider knowledge, we reopened our mom's medical record. The crystals were hand-written as a side note, the night before she passed."

These crystal-like inclusions are blue-green in color, refractile, and found in the cytoplasm of neutrophils. Their presence after liver injuries caused people to believe they were composed of bile. Later studies showed they are a lipid product, not an acid.

Dr. Kudela theorized the crystals form after acute damage to multiple organs. Unlike his peers, he knew the only injury that led to crystal development one hundred percent of the time. He also knew there wasn't a laboratory test at Drivers to detect it.

"I'm sorry for your loss. I appreciate you sharing that with me." Andy offered a soft smile. "Are you trying to theorize a mechanism of formation, or is this going to be a collection of case studies?"

"Neither. Both?" They shared a laugh. "We know their association with lactic acidosis. We know things like sepsis, hepatic or liver injury, heart attacks, certain cancers, like AML, can lead to metabolic disorders. However, the crystals don't develop every time. While their sixty percent morbidity rate seems high, the crystals are not present in the majority of people who pass away from these conditions."

"You're trying to find another underlying factor?"

"Exactly. To be honest, Dr. Sanders thinks their nickname causes more sensationalism than they've earned, and I'm wasting my time."

"Dr. Sanders won't review requests if they have the wrong name. They must be noted as blue-green neutrophilic inclusions. If he's in the lab, we're not even allowed to say the words," Andy leaned in, "Death Crystals."

Chapter 6

Current Day

"AND HOW DID THAT make you feel? Knowing you are part of the problem?" Felice raises her eyebrows.

"I'm getting a lot of mixed signals from you. You tell me this isn't therapy. Yet you one hundred percent stole that line from one of my sessions. You made fun of me for wanting warm water, but I can see the steam rising from your cup."

Felice did not move.

Ryker rode the silence for a minute. As far as interrogations go, two people in a dark room, sharing a comforting beverage, things could be much worse.

"When you're in a meeting, do you look at who's talking, or who's being talkinged to?" Felice might lock Ryker in some weird, you-know-too-much jail for the rest of her life, but Ryker needed validation. She can't be the only person who looks the enemy directly in their face.

"Who's being talkinged to."

"Nice." Ryker leans in for a high five.

"Is one of the worst grammatical endings to a sentence I've heard in a long time."

"Lame."

"However, the act of listening is more nuanced than maintaining eye contact with the speaker."

"You can agree with me and continue to hate my word choice. That's called cognitive dissonance." Ryker shoots an imaginary basketball. "The therap-ee has become the therap-ist."

Tuesday: Nine Days Ago

THE EDGE OF A bookcase greeted people as they entered his office. The shelves expanded the length of the wall to the opposite corner, adorned with reference books, trinkets, and photos of his French Bulldog. Ryker and Elyssa sat in two chairs, smooshed together against a window, opposite their boss. On his desk was an amber, antique glass dish filled with red hard candies.

"Help yourselves to a piece, it's homemade," Liam said.

Elyssa, a suspected people pleaser, took one without question. Come to think of it, it was the first food Ryker saw Elyssa partake.

"No thanks," Ryker said, attempting to sound casual. The color was wrong. It looked like old cough drops. Plus, they were in trouble. Why give Liam any satisfaction? "Did you guys see Dr. Kudela?"

Liam and Elyssa exchanged glances. It was clear they did not understand.

"He kept sticking his tongue out while I was talking. Tell me I wasn't the only person who noticed it?" Ryker wanted to call him out on it during the meeting. Was he trying to intimidate her? Make her uncomfortable? It could be due to a medical condition. Being an asshole is not the same as being a bully.

"I was looking at you when you spoke," Liam said.

"I thought it was polite to look at the speaker," Elyssa said. "Have I been doing meetings wrong?"

"Yeah." Ryker cracked her thumb knuckle against her index finger. "When you're convening with the enemy, you maintain eye contact. No matter who's talking. Gage their sincerity."

"I was unaware of this practice. Noted for future sessions." Elyssa laughed.

"I didn't know Dr. Sanders was the enemy." Liam's statement doubled as a question.

"He's our boss." Ryker opted stop there. While talking to her boss.

A knock on the open door interrupted the lighthearted mood. Fatima, the new first shift supervisor, quality control expert, and a specialist in blood banking, stood unamused. "Are you all busy?"

"We're waiting on you," Liam answered.

Busy? Ryker knew her face matched her level of confusion. She was also well aware that her confused face and her angry face looked very similar. They are the same. Confusion makes Ryker's brain angry.

Fatima closed the door behind her and worked her way next to Liam. There was not enough room for another chair, so she remained standing. "Will you please tell me what happened last night? How did we miss irradiating that unit?"

"Are you serious? We killed." Ryker spoke on instinct. "First shift missed the blood type. They missed adding the sickle cell instructions. They missed adding the irradiation requirement. One unit wasn't updated in the LIS. I don't know how, but at least it was irradiated. Unlike all the units you had first shift set up."

Offense was the wrong tactic.

"O negative, antigen negative units would have been as safe, if not safer, than the O pos you gave."

"It would have put us below minimum inventory, ABI couldn't replace them. If we did things your way, we'd be triaging every order for O neg patients right now. And. Those units weren't irradiated. That is also FDA reportable."

Liam held up his hand, "The intention of this meeting was not to place blame. I have a theory of how the error occurred, but I wanted to verify with the two of you."

Fatima folded her arms.

Ryker leaned back in the chair and crossed her ankles.

"We irradiated the units in batches." Elyssa offered an olive branch.

"We know that, we can only fit three at a time in the machine." Fatima increased her cadence. As if faster equated to smarter.

"Instead of us guessing what you need to know, can you ask a more specific question? Something other than *what happened*?" Ryker asked. She caught, and somewhat stopped herself from rolling her eyes.

"Yes. Thank you." Liam nodded toward Fatima like he was telling her Ryker could cooperate. "Were the units crossmatched before you added the instruction?"

"Yes." Ryker uncrossed her legs and sat straight. She drew in a long breath. "They were crossmatched when Regina got here. She said they needed irradiation. I verified the red cell order. I added the requirement. Then we," she gestured to Elyssa and herself, "irradiated the units."

"That's how you did it. The LIS only checks the requirements at crossmatch. That's why it didn't flag you on the missed unit." Liam made a note on his yellow pad of paper.

"Who taught you to irradiate while crossmatched?" Fatima wasn't done with the fight.

"I knew how to do it. There's nothing written in the policy that forbids it. It seemed more efficient." Ryker was a superuser for the LIS. She'd used it at her previous hospital and helped train the first stock of techs at Drivers. Too much knowledge can be a dangerous thing.

"It's not more efficient if it puts the patient at risk." Fatima leaned forward.

"Are you going to talk to the person who failed to add the requirements? Or who crossmatched an entire batch of non-irradiated units?" Elyssa asked. Ryker was grateful for the backup.

"We've already spoken to first shift," Liam said.

"How is this a bigger deal than Quinneth ignoring mixed field. Twice. I told you weeks ago she doesn't know what she's doing. Y'all pushed her through training. Now her mistakes are impacting me and Elyssa. She could have harmed a patient."

"Which one of those things is worse for you?" Fatima asked. "Like Dr. Sanders, Liam, and now I am saying, there was no patient harm. Again, Ryker, this meeting is not about blame."

"You tossing that sentence on the floor doesn't mean you stand by it." Ryker's eyes narrowed. *If she wants a fight, fuck it, let's fight.*

Fatima's face flushed as she inhaled a quick, deep breath.

"I think we're done here," Liam said as he stood. "Thank you, both."

Fatima wasn't moving. Ryker struggled to inch her chair backwards so she could straighten her legs. The heat of frustration and embarrassment overwhelmed her ability to move with ease. Thud. Elyssa tripped over Ryker's chair and fell onto Liam's desk. Her face the same color as the terrible candy that flew out of her mouth, landing on Liam's yellow notepad.

"To be fair," Elyssa said after a successful second attempt to exit, and they were out of supervisor earshot. "Drivers doesn't have a chair competency."

Alone in the storage room, Ryker inhaled for four seconds, held her breath for four seconds, and released for four seconds. *Shit.* She repeated the breaths. *I can do this.*

An antibody identification worksheet waited in front of the manual rack with a sample. Not too bad. The longer Ryker reviewed the work done by Quinneth, the more questions she had. First time positive antibody screen. Quinneth performed an eleven-cell panel with an auto control. Correct. The patient reacted to all the cells with a homozygous Duffy B antigen. Autocontrol negative. Instead of utilizing her own brain, Quinneth relied on the machine to think for her. She ran an eleven-cell enzyme panel.

The enzyme panel enhances antigenic activity on the Rh, Kell, or Kidd systems. Problem one, it destroys Duffy antigens. Problem two, it takes forty minutes to run, and was completely negative. This should have been a bigger hint towards the anti-Duffy B antibody. Alas, she did not take the bait. In the time it took her to run that test, she could have ruled out the remaining alloantibodies.

"Ryker, are you working on a patient, Cortez?" June shouted from desk.

"Yes."

"The nurse wants to know how long until the blood is available."

"I don't have a blood order."

"I see it in the computer."

"Tell her at least two hours, I'll call her when it's ready."

Verifying for herself, June was correct. There was an order for two units of blood. STAT. *Fuck.* Using what she could on the enzyme panel, Ryker needed to rule out two more antibodies: M and S. She was lucky. One cell to rule out them all: Duffy B negative, M homozygous positive, S homozygous positive.

After dripping her cells, she placed the gel card in the incubator and set a fifteen-minute timer. Step two, find the red cell order. June said it wasn't up front. Ryker double-checked. Nope. Remembering where Quinneth sat, she sifted through her shred bin. There it was, along with the original type and screen order.

The red cell order printed at 1100. Type and screen received at 1123. Antibody screen answered positive at 1230. Drivers policy requires resident notification for any red blood cell order that will take longer than two hours to fill. Quinneth should have notified the resident at 1230. Was required to notify them at 1330, before second shift started. With all the fucking meetings, it was now 1630.

"I paged the resident," Ryker said aloud, to anyone listening. Searching for Duffy B negative units prior to finishing rule-outs was tempting. *Don't jump ahead.* If it wasn't an anti-Duffy B, she'd be wasting more time.

The phone rang. The outside line looked like the resident's number. Ryker snatched it on the first ring.

"Transfusion, this is Ryker, how may I help you...FDA...Give me a moment to make sure my supervisor is in her office before I transfer you...She's there, her name is Yvette, I am transferring you now."

Not my problem.

Another call. Ryker hesitated.

"Transfusion, this is Ryker, how may I help you...Hi Dr. Kudela, I have a patient in the ED with two units of red blood cells ordered, they have a new antibody. I'm calling for an RBC delay...XXXXXX, last name Channar...Thank you."

Ryker documented the triage in the patient's chart. The fifteen-minute timer beeped. Card nested in the centrifuge, she set another timer for ten minutes. Enough time to fill out an incident report.

As new people filter in, they tend to make the same mistakes. Sometimes you get a unicorn like Quinneth who screws things up in ways you couldn't imagine. As she found mistakes, Ryker would address them with new employees. That led to one or three of them telling Liam she was too intimidating. The solution, Ryker should not address the training tech. She could address the senior tech training them. That escalated to Ryker emailing the supervisor of the training tech. The supervisor would address Ryker's concerns if they deemed it necessary. That turned out to be fucking useless. Ryker took it upon herself to develop her own solution. If it's annoying but not impactful, let it go. If it's annoying and impactful, write an incident report.

To her surprise, this new plan of action worked. Was Fatima tossing most of the reports into the shred bin? Probably. Did Ryker keep a copy of all the reports she made? Nope. Was anything going to get corrected? Who knows. Folding the reports into a crisp square, evidence attached, dropping them into the metal lock box, and hearing the thud of passive justice felt good.

Ten-minute timer up. The final cell was negative. Ryker triple checked the patient was eligible for phenotype testing. No blood products within three months at Drivers, none listed in SAGA.

To make an alloantibody, a person's red cells must be negative for that specific antigen. People with type A blood can receive type O blood because they have the O antigen. Conversely, people with type O blood are negative for the A antigen and cannot receive that blood due to natural antibodies.

Routine testing for minor blood group antigens is not necessary. Humans are not born with antibodies to the minor blood groups. Most people who are Duffy B negative can receive Duffy B positive blood and will not develop an anti-Duffy B. Once an antibody develops, the blood bank tests for that specific antigen. Antigen-negative blood is given for all future transfusions. An O pos person with an anti-Duffy B would receive type O, Duffy B negative blood.

Ryker took the anti-Duffy B antisera out of the fridge. Reaching for test tubes, her hand hit cardboard. Extra supplies under the desk? Empty. *God damn first shift*. Ryker stole the box of tubes from the student area. She promised herself she'd refill both before the end of the night. She labeled a glass tube with "Fyb" and the patient's initials. One drop of antisera. One drop of patient red cells. Spin. The red cell button at the bottom of the tube dispersed. Duffy B negative.

Now to find blood. There weren't any ready, free-use Duffy B negatives available. Ryker removed segments from 10 random units of type-compatible blood.

"They sent the pickup."

Ryker twitched, fumbling the sleeve of units.

"Sorry about that," Elyssa said, her hand covering her laugh. "Tough antibody got you deep in thought?"

"No. It's a straightforward Duffy B. Quinneth should have completed it before we got here. I was debating whether I could wait to go pee after testing the units or if I should go before."

"It's a real Sophie's choice." Elyssa handed Ryker the request.

"That jump scare decided for me. I'll be right back." Ryker tossed the units in the fridge and put the request on her desk.

A dark yellow, earthy-scented stream told Ryker she needed to drink water. Now she brings in a two-liter bottle she fills from home. Regina was in the breakroom having coffee with Yvette.

"Are you staying late again?" Ryker asked. The apheresis clinic closes at 1600. Regina is the only nurse currently qualified to take call in her department. The new hires aren't experienced enough.

"You in charge of payroll?" Regina smiled, but Ryker knew that was a hint to mind her business.

"Regina and I were talking about that exchange last night." Yvette stirred the light brown liquid in her cup. The room smelled amazing.

"Dr. Sanders tried to streamline things, then Fatima gets involved and complicates it." Ryker sipped from her straw.

"I don't know about all that." Regina shared a look with Yvette. "I do know, in all my years treating people in sickle cell crisis, I've never had one tell me a demon was after him."

"Wow. What do you do for that?" Ryker asked.

"Pain takes people out of their right minds." Regina rested her spoon on a napkin. "I asked if he wanted to speak to a chaplain. Young man said it wouldn't do any good. Also said I was wasting all this blood, the demon was going to take it from him."

"What about a psych consult?" Yvette asked.

"Dr. Kudela said he didn't want to flag their chart. It might cause other providers to think they were dramatizing symptoms for meds."

"I'm guessing you added a note anyway?" Ryker thought about pulling out a chair. As she approached, unwelcoming eyes darted towards the empty seat.

"Of course I did. Along with Kudela's recommendation."

"Nice." Ryker leaned in, anticipating more information.

Regina and Yvette sipped their coffees in a pause of silence.

Hint taken. "Have a good night, Regina."

Back in the lab and feeling refreshed, Ryker got to work. Ten labeled glass tubes, a drop of anti-Duffy B antisera in each tube, a drop of red cells, and spin. Twenty seconds later, the first unit was

Duffy B negative. *Sweet.* Second unit, also Duffy B negative. *High five.* Some days, Ryker might have stopped there. She found the units she needed. Why test the other eight? Sunny's disapproval face tsk-tsked in Ryker's head.

Ugh. Fine. In honor of Sunny, Ryker continued. Unit three, negative. *Weird.* Unit four, negative. *Suspicious.* All ten units, negative for Duffy B antigen. *Unpossible.* Antigen frequency is well documented. Charts, mathematical equations, and online calculators tell techs how many units to screen to find antigen-negative blood. Depending on the donor population, twenty to eighty percent of the units should be positive for Duffy B. Could Ryker have selected ten magically negative units? Yes. Is it likely? Absolutely not.

One major difference between new techs and seasoned techs, learning to tell the difference between normal weird and bad weird. Had one of those units been positive, Ryker would have let it go. All negative? Something is wrong.

Label, label. Drip the antisera. Drip a known positive. Drip a known negative. Spin. Both were negative. *Fuck.* Double-check panel, choose a different heterozygous positive cell. Repeat testing. Results, all negative. *Double fuck.* Ryker drew an 'X' over the face label of the vial in black marker. *The antisera is contaminated. Don't panic.*

The fridge in the storage room housed the unopened bottles of antisera. Another bottle, the same lot number, was available. She dripped her controls. Results were valid, one positive and one negative. *Finally.*

First, she needed to re-test the patient's red cells. Negative. *Okay. Okay.* Moving on to the units. The first two tested negative, Ryker held her breath with the third. Positive. Exhale. Units four through six, and eight through ten, also positive. That added up. She put her results in the LIS and started crossmatching.

Not wanting to conduct a full investigation on an empty stomach, Ryker opted for a Teams message to Yvette. "The opened vial of anti-Duffy B didn't pass QC. It was used for testing this morning. I found another vial that did work. Do I need to repeat any of those earlier tests? No rush." Crossmatches take about forty minutes on the machine. Yes, Ryker could have done them manually, saved about ten minutes. However, the delay was called, automation is the preferred testing method, and she was starved.

Chapter 7

Wednesday: Eight Days Ago, 1700

BETWEEN THE TENSION FROM the inspection and Fatima's email, Ryker needed a pick-me-up for lunch. Rice and beans wouldn't give her the serotonin boost required to finish this shift. Tonight deserved a trip to the mini mart. Thanksgiving Dinner propaganda covered the atrium. In her five years at Drivers, the most they'd ever done for the fall was a table of pumpkins outside the gift shop.

This year, any surface that could support a gourd held at least three. One always decorated with tail feathers, eyes, a beak, and a wattle. Cornucopias filled with Drivers swag and wrapped in cellophane sat in dozens of windowsills. Four-foot-tall floor signs replicating the official invitation stood in every elevator bank. An odd size for a turkey. It made it appear more menacing than quirky. To drive home the horror vibes, a seven-foot turkey greeted people at the entrance of the cafeteria holding a knife and fork, napkin draped around its neck. Occasionally, someone snuck a golden Pi pen or Pi sticker in with the decorations. Drivers requested employees report any decor vandalism to the new dedicated phone line.

Halloween night, 2200. An email was sent to "Drivers All," from DriversPost, the hospital email system. The image, a turkey in lingerie, big flirty eyelashes, stockings, and a pilgrim hat. A dialog bubble read, "Get Stuffed."

Next to the flirty turkey was an outline of a cooked turkey resting on a platter. Inside the cooked turkey, "Tuesday, November 26 @ 6 pm."

The body of the email read, "Please join us in the Drivers dining room for an all-you-can-eat buffet! We're celebrating our Heroes with fun and games and remembering those we've lost with a tasty PowerPoint. Bring the kids. Mingle with loved ones of coworkers you killed to survive. Show that never say die, Drivers spirit." This was not a Drivers approved email. Ryker printed two copies. One to frame, and one to send to Sunny.

The next morning, November 1, 0700, human resources emailed the real announcement. Drivers would be hosting a Thanksgiving Hero and Memorial Dinner for all employees and special guests. A week later, another email clarified the dinner was one meal per person, not an all-you-can-eat buffet. "While children are welcome, we do not have the space for carnival games. Some people may have been misinformed."

Happy with her mini mart loot, Ryker took the stairs back to the breakroom. She set her dinner, vindaloo chicken, a white chocolate macadamia nut cookie, and a diet Dr. Pepper in the bookcase. Bathrooms should have a biohazard sign. Food and drinks do not go over the threshold.

The bathroom was dark. She pressed the light switch. The door closed behind her. Still dark.

Fuck. Stay calm. There aren't any monsters in here.

She pressed the switch again. Lights on.

She blinked twice.

She turned the lights off. Deep breath. Lights on.

"Holy fuck," she yelled.

The slumped body remained on the floor.

"Holy fuck," she said.

Hospital lighting is no one's friend, but the victim was not this pale earlier today.

"Holy fuck," she whispered.

The body didn't respond to her zombie test.

There, on the neck, two small puncture wounds, an inch and a half apart. A dry trickle of blood led from the wounds to the floor. She waited for a rise in the victim's chest. Hovered her hand over the victim's mouth to feel for breath. Nothing.

Holy fuck. I could've been peeing during a murder.

Current Day

"Which did you choose?" Felice has exemplary posture. The walls could burst into flames and that pristine silhouette would still be the most intimidating thing in the room.

"I called the non-emergency line. She was already dead."

"How did that go?"

Ryker laughs, "Oh my god, they were pissed. I had two people yelling into the phone telling me to call 911."

Wednesday: Eight Days Ago, 1720

The cops, well cop, took longer than Ryker expected for an emergency. Balding and overweight, he sauntered down the hallway like he had better things to do with his night.

"There's a body in here," Officer Whyte shouted as the door automatically closed behind him.

"There's a dead body in there," he restated as he struggled to find a way to prop the door open.

"That's why I called." Ryker waited for instructions.

"Why isn't there an EMT?" Officer Whyte released the door, letting it slam.

"I called 911. I told them someone was on the floor in the bathroom, and I was pretty sure they're dead. I thought they would inform whoever needed to come."

At that moment, two nurses with stethoscopes turned the corner. They wore matching purple Drivers sweatshirts.

"Did someone call for medical assistance?" The taller of the two asked.

Officer Whyte gave Ryker a hard stare, as if this proved she was fault for their miscommunication.

"There's a woman on the floor in there," Officer Whyte stated, like he discovered the body.

"She's dead." Ryker clarified.

"Dead?" The tall nurse asked, walking into the restroom.

The body lay as cold and motionless as Ryker found it.

"Is this an employee?" The tall nurse walked around the body, "We can't take vitals on employees."

"She's an FDA inspector. I guess that makes her a visitor."

The tall nurse knelt near her wrist to check for a pulse. "She's dead."

"That's what I said on the phone," Ryker said, allowing her frustration to be heard.

"What do you want us to do?" The shorter nurse asked Ryker.

"I don't know what to do. That's why I called 911." It's not like she found a kitten on the side of the road. There's no dead body distribution system.

While they were talking, Officer Whyte was on his phone. Finally doing his job. "I called this into the office. They're sending a coroner and a detective. You ladies can leave." A clammy hand touched Ryker's shoulder. "Not you, I have to ask you some questions."

Sigh. Ryker already answered so many questions today. This wasn't going to go well. "Can I let my department know first? My lunch ended five minutes ago."

Officer Whyte agreed, on the premise he would escort Ryker into the lab. She gave a more thorough explanation of the phone call and Eva's present condition. Liam and Dr. Sanders laid their inspection reports aside.

"You're sure she was dead?" Officer Whyte sat at what used to be Lonnie's desk. He helped himself to a donut. "Am I bothering you?"

Ryker thought she hid her face better. "You're the third person to ask me that. Yes. I'm sure. The number one qualification for a biologist is the ability to tell the difference between the living and the dead." She repeated the phrase with the same snobbery as her college ecology professor who coined it.

"Okay. She was dead. How long did you know her?" The officer scribbled in his flipbook.

"I didn't know her. I became aware of her existence at 1457." Ryker wondered if those little books were part of the uniform or if he used it to twin his favorite tv cop. Like how everyone in her deployment group bought pocketknives and Leathermans to bring to Afghanistan.

"You were on your way to the bathroom when you saw the victim walk in first?"

"Yes."

"But you didn't follow her inside?"

"No."

"Why not?"

"I was worried she would talk to me."

"Wow. She might be alive if you went in."

"Or we could both be dead."

"If that makes you feel better."

Fuck you.

The longer they sat, the more frustrated Ryker became with his style of questions. Did you notice this? Exactly what? Exactly When? She reported a dead body. They wanted her to explain a murder. That's what you get for trying to be polite. She'd already told him the whole story, in painstaking detail. Well, not all of it. She left out the neck wound. She was pretty sure she knew who the killer was. Not who. More like what the killer was.

"We'll call you in the morning if we need more information." The officer flipped his book closed.

"Can you make a note not to call before eleven?"

The officer agreed, but he didn't write it down. Perhaps his book was at maximum information capacity.

Wednesday: Eight Days Ago, 2100

THE MICROWAVE CHIMED. CLOCKING out asks if you had thirty minutes of an uninterrupted break. Ryker was going to say yes, and it was going to be the truth.

Sauce from the vindaloo chicken coated her mouth. The corners of her lips burned. Ryker took one of the emergency antacids she kept in her lunch bag. Spicy food wasn't the only thing causing discomfort.

The first bite of her cookie tasted like it would make the night go better. By the end of the pancake-sized treat, her stomach bloated. Her body felt gross, her brain wouldn't stop yelling at her, and the tingle of acid reflux crept into her chest. *It's how you deserve to feel. She might be alive if you were nicer.*

Ryker inhaled for a count of four, held that in for a four count, and exhaled as long as she could. She repeated the breathing exercise until the wave of self-pity retreated. *You did not kill her.* Checking the time on her phone. Thirty-four minutes. *Selfish. That's why the SSB didn't want you. That's why no one wants to work with you. No. No. Deep breath in, hold, deep breath out.*

Automated offered plenty of distractions. Both machines were out of gel cards. She loaded more and refilled the empty system liquid container. She'd been ignoring it since she took over this afternoon.

Each machine has two. If the second one runs out, the machine pauses, not explodes.

"I thought you were joking when you said problems tend to find you."

Ryker jumped. A welcome startle.

Elyssa hovered as Ryker started her samples, "Of all the people to stumble into a body, it's like they were trying to set you up."

"Right? Thank you," Ryker said, not taking her eyes off the display panel to ensure the tests started. "I mean, Eva did get the worst end of it."

Elyssa fought back a laugh, "Did you hear anything about those event reports? You did one for a delay, and what was the other one?"

"The contaminated anti-Duffy B. I didn't *hear* anything. I read a dissertation describing how wrong I was. Quinneth did her best. And the antisera worked earlier that morning, so I need to be more careful."

"What?" Elyssa shook her head. "She blamed you for contaminating the reagents? That's crazy."

"Right? I knew it was Quinneth. I checked the completed tests. She was the last person to use it. All I did was ask if it was necessary to repeat the testing. I didn't even say whose tests."

"That's such bs. Quinneth is becoming more of a liability than anything. They just don't want to admit it. I'd say she's setting you up on purpose, but she isn't smart enough." Elyssa laughed. A carrier dropped into the tube station.

Ryker opened the email from Fatima. She hadn't been able to read the entire thing on her first attempt. Rage built with each progressive sentence. If she didn't walk away from it, she might have responded in ways she would regret. Now, with Elyssa's validation in mind, she wanted to read it again. Still bullshit, but perhaps the tone wasn't quite as harsh as her initial read.

Fatima recognized the missed triage, but defended Quinneth's testing methods. Then, Fatima went on a rant about an anti-N antibody that Ryker and Yvette failed to identify last week.

"We didn't fail." Ryker typed, "We suspected it was an anti-N, but prior to the new reagents, Drivers never had one react at IgG. Not to mention, it didn't react on all the homozygous N positive cells. We called it a nonspecific antibody. Drivers considers anti-N clinically insignificant. A nonspecific antibody allowed for gel crossmatching. We thought it was the safer option until you had the chance to review it." Ryker closed the email without sending.

Since showing up as Liam's saving grace, Fatima has been a nightmare. Asking her a question is the same as questioning her intelligence. Seeking clarity is accusing her of not following policy. Asking for policy updates for the changes she's sent out via email is accusing her of doing nothing all day.

At least she could walk away from email. Emails rarely got Ryker into trouble.

As a med tech, losing track of time is a jarring sensation. It's like your brain was aimlessly wandering through a pasture before it walked directly into an electric fence. *How long ago did I start that run?* She checked the timer, it was still on twenty minutes. *Shit.* Based on the turnaround times, her samples finished a while ago. One of them had only three more minutes to meet its ninety-minute goal.

Four ABORhs waited for approval in the LIS. No antibody screens. One minute left, she checked the analyzer's result menu. In bold letters across all four antibody screens, "QC FAIL."

"What? Why?" Ryker shouted at the taunting all caps. "You had QC this morning."

A few more clicks revealed the answer. Someone loaded a new lot number of screening cells at 1458. Hoping she caught Quinneth red-handed, Ryker unloaded the reagents.

In the load/ unload shelf of the analyzer sat six glass vials. A trio of empty screen cells, one, two, and three, of the lot number that was QC'd this morning. Elyssa's initials and yesterday's date written on the side of the label. The other three were full. Of course, they didn't have an open date and initials. If Quinneth had done it correctly, she might have realized she loaded the wrong lot number. This lot wasn't in use yet.

Ryker went to the reagent fridge, "Oh, fuck you." Refrigerators aren't offended by profanity. "We're out of screen cells? Why didn't they change lot numbers when they did QC? Why wasn't this on the shift report? June, Elyssa did you notice the screen cells were low this week?"

"It wasn't me," June shouted back.

"I wasn't accusing you," Ryker said, in a tone that didn't support her argument.

"What do you need?" Elyssa asked.

"Can you load those samples on the other machine while I run QC on this one?"

"Do you want me to grab an incident report for you?" Elyssa smiled.

As funny as the slogan, "Another day, another incident report," sounded the first time she said it, Ryker worried the universe interpreted it as a challenge. Is sarcasm the same as manifesting?

Chapter 8

WHEN SHE THOUGHT OF working for a secret government agency that takes down supernatural creatures, this was not it. A Men in Black style training regime with obstacle courses featuring zombies that pop up and you bash in the head. A sleek, blond-haired elf fight instructor who could shoot a coin out of the air with an arrow. Plating ghost ectoplasm to see what kind of bacteria live in the spirit world. Bigfoot parasitology. Not logging in samples.

Samples came from different places. She couldn't tell from where, but each label had different formatting. Various ways of assigning accession numbers. Some came with handwritten collection information. Some did not. Gladson timed her as she verified three patient identifiers: name, medical record number, and date of birth. Faster than thirty seconds, he'd comment. "Rushing receiving makes for sloppy clean up."

The lab portion of the business building they were in had blackout screens over all the windows. No one could see in or out. She thought she recognized most of the analyzers. She wasn't allowed to venture to the back. When she asked, Gladson said, "Ah, yes. The coveted tour. That isn't part of front desk training."

People dropping off samples all wore back scrubs. They handed the bags to Gladson. He removed the papers inside the bag, compared them to the samples, then gave the samples to Sunny. After scanning, Sunny listened to his critiques. Once he finished speaking at her, Gladson reclaimed the samples. He placed them into a boring black rectangular basket and took them to another room. Anytime Sunny turned her head to scope out the lab behind her, Gladson intervened with conversation.

"Do you like to cook?" He asked.

Sunny was trying to figure out what they stored in the fridges. Zombie brain matter? Space creature sputum? Probably something lame like reagents.

"I noticed you brought your lunch," Gladson said, louder this time.

"Oh, um, sure, I like to meal prep. If I'm feeling zesty, I'll bake some cookies or brownies."

"How do you organize your recipes?"

"I, uh, I never thought about that. I don't use recipes too often, so I don't have a system for organizing them."

"You meal prep without a recipe?"

"I put seasoning on my chicken and put it in the skillet. I have a rice maker and I use frozen green beans."

"I've got a great recipe for a chicken and rice casserole." He smacked his lips and rubbed his stomach.

"I don't really do casseroles." She turned her head away from the uncomfortable body language.

"You'd love this one, it's chicken, rice, broccoli, and cheese." He held out the word cheese and pretended to drool.

"Do you cook the chicken first, so it gets a nice crisp on the skin?"

"No. That's the beauty of it. It all goes in one pot, gets baked in the oven."

Sounds like horrible, unflavored mush.

"My friend Catherine would've enjoyed it," Sunny said.

I don't want to yuck his food, but how do I be nice without ending up with this recipe?

Luckily, another boring human guy in black scrubs came by with a lunchbox full of samples. This lab had a cut-out window. Like all the other boring labs, it faced a plain white wall. At least Drivers had art.

"Ah, good," Gladson clasped his hands and rubbed them together. "Having so many at once will be a little challenge."

It was not a challenge. Sunny put on her happy face. Taking her time inspecting each sample.

"Are you sure all of them checked out?" He asked as if he expected a specific response.

"The label was a little short on one. The first letter of the last name was clipped. It's clearly a *T*." She held the sample in question. "It meets our requirements."

"Great," he said with unironic enthusiasm. "You wouldn't believe how many people sit at my window and miss those things. Yes. We will accept that sample, but it's important to notice. I'm so glad you caught that."

"Don't you mean glad, son?" Sunny waited for the laugh.

"I just thought of something. I'm so glad, son, you caught that. Like my name. Gladson."

Sunny tilted her head to the side.

"Don't worry. My jokes go over people's heads all time." Now he laughed. "Oh, here comes another batch. Let's get our focus caps on." He mimed putting on a hat. "That's just me being silly again."

THREE FULL DAYS OF examining and scanning specimen labels. The morning of the fourth day, Sunny parked in a secluded area and let herself cry. "I gave up everything I knew, for this?" she asked herself through sobs. To her red-eyed reflection in the rearview mirror, she added, "Finish this week. One week is not forever."

Again, she sat at the desk, and again, someone in black scrubs dropped off a bag of samples. To her surprise, Gladson handed Sunny the entire bag. "I know it's a big step, but I think you're ready to review the packing lists. It's similar to reviewing specimen labels. Make sure everything on the list is in the bag and everything in the bag is on the list."

"Okay." Sunny sat up straight, "What do we do if the list and the samples don't match?"

Gladson shook his head, "It goes through a two-tech check before coming to us."

"That doesn't answer my question. Do we call someone? How do we find missing samples?"

"Missing samples?" Gladson clutched his chest. "I don't know where you worked before, but here we rely on the Swiss cheese method."

Sunny shrugged.

"I can't believe you haven't heard of the Swiss cheese method. It's great, you'll love it. You see, one person is like one slice of Swiss cheese. If only one person does a task, something can slip through their holes."

Sunny bit her cheek.

"But if you stack slices of Swiss together, they fill each other's holes. Isn't that a perfect analogy?"

An orgy of efficiency.

"What if there isn't enough overlap. Leaving a tiny, unfilled hole?" Sunny asked.

"Procedure and methodology acts as a plug to help shrink holes others might miss."

That's not how those plugs work.

Sunny verified the packing list matched all the samples. Verified all the labels were acceptable. "These are good."

"Have you thought any more about organizing your recipes?" Gladson asked when he returned from dropping off the samples.

"Nope. I was all done thinking about it." Conversation flows because two people keep saying what they want to say about a subject. Sunny does not have to be directed or asked to continue her thoughts. Over the week, Gladson had a strange habit of asking Sunny questions he wished she would ask him.

"How do you organize your recipes?" It made Sunny uncomfortable repeating Gladson like a parrot, but it appeased him.

"Ahhh, that's the problem. I want to write a program to search through my recipes, so I don't have to scroll through file names."

"What about control F? Doesn't that find words for you?"

"Are you talking about in a Word document?"

The note of condescension made Sunny hesitate. "It works in other things, too."

"What I want to make is far more advanced than that. But no one has invented the search program I want."

"Why don't you invent it yourself?" Sunny tried to sound supportive.

"That's the problem. I keep telling you, I don't know how I want to organize them, so I can't figure out how I want to search them."

"You could sort them by meal types, breakfast, lunch, dinner, and desserts. Then make your program. If you don't like how it's organized, you can switch it up."

"Wow. You really don't know anything about programming. I'll just keep playing it in my head like a song. Speaking of, what's your favorite type of music?"

Ignoring the casual insult, Sunny welcomed a change of topic. However, she hated these kinds of questions. She loved music. Her favorite? Absolute favorite? She's never sorted that out. It's too hard. Too many options. Too many moods. Different music goes with different moods. What if she tells him one thing now, and four months from now her favorite changes? Does that make her a liar?

"I don't know if I have a favorite. I still listen to lots of nineties and two thousands stuff. Current music, I like Billie Eilish."

"So you use Spotify?"

Typical follow-up question from Gladson. The kind that makes Sunny think he isn't trying to get to know her at all. He just wants to hear himself talk. There was no need to put all that effort into answering, the answer was irrelevant.

"Sure. I guess you do?"

"It's just," he sighed. "I find it difficult to describe the music I like. It's not like anything on the radio. I've spent centuries collecting songs. I've finally curated the perfect playlist that encapsulates my musical tastes. Could I send it to you?"

At work, Sunny is forced into extrovert mode. If they were at a coffee shop, she would not be engaging with a stranger. She would be in her car. If she can't do the drive-through, she goes to a different coffee shop. At work, especially at a new job, Sunny often finds herself in conversations she doesn't know how to navigate. Sharing information she regrets. Agreeing to things that make her uncomfortable.

"Sounds neat."

WITH THE FIRST GROUP of specimens the next day, Gladson told Sunny she was ready to start processing. Instead of dropping off the samples, he took her into the room. A tech she hadn't met was at the freezer. She tied her dark brown hair into a neat bun. Eyeliner, a nose ring, and a bright pink undershirt completed her outfit.

"I trust you checked those samples out in the computer?" Gladson asked.

"I trust you're being appropriately nice to the new hire?" She asked without looking at him. "We haven't met."

"I'm Sunny," she said as she extended her hand.

"Everyone here calls me Nevasha." She held her hand up in a wave. "Handshakes are for inspectors."

"That's badass," Sunny pointed to the tattoo on Nevasha's right arm. The tail of a black and grey snake started at her wrist and wrapped upwards to her bicep. Instead of a head, a bunch of small purple flowers bloomed. "I've got a couple myself." Sunny pulled up her long sleeves. No one stated they weren't allowed to show tattoos or wear any color undershirts other than white. Sunny liked to choose when and how she stood out from the crowd.

"That's sick. Maybe we can swap stories, sometime." Nevasha smiled at Sunny. She also smiled at Gladson, but it was different. Sunny made a mental note to ask what that was about. It was nice to meet someone with a similar vibe. Sunny's skin felt better. The air wasn't so itchy.

"I didn't realize you had ink under there," Gladson emphasized the word ink, as if he was disgusted by it.

"Uh, yeah, do you have any?" She knew he didn't. Gladson rolled his eyes when she complimented Nevasha's snake.

"No. You know, I can never think of anything I like enough to be on me forever."

"Maybe you haven't found the right recipe." That's what happens when she gets a little comfortable. Without thinking, Sunny made a joke.

"I just thought of the funniest thing. What if I got a tattoo of my chicken casserole recipe? I bet no one's ever done that before."

"You might be the first." Sunny gave him the fake laugh he was waiting for. "So how do we process these bad boys?"

The answer, boring. Sunny hoped to learn something new. Top secret ways to keep samples viable for longer periods. Additives only available to the government. Instead, it was more of the same. Most of the samples did not require testing in the lab. They were sent for long-term storage. Every sample that came through the lab was stored in a freezer. Print label, handwrite the date and initial, place on plastic storage tube. Add sample, cap, give to Gladson for review.

After two hours of error-free processing, Gladson deemed Sunny competent enough to store the samples.

"It's a basic LIS," Gladson said as he moved the computer mouse. "The storage component keeps track of where samples are, and in which freezer. The whole blood samples go in the ultra cold -80 °C, the others go in the -15 °C freezers. After the samples are stored, the patient charts are reviewed. Additional testing may be requested depending on the samples we were able to get." A straightforward process. Gladson spent thirty minutes explaining it before he let Sunny try her first sample.

He leaned in closer than she preferred as she navigated the LIS. There was a HIPAA screen on the monitor, on all the monitors, preventing peekers from side glancing.

"Sample processing is as integral a part of the SSB as field work. Speaking of, did you get a chance to listen to that playlist?" Gladson asked. He closed his eyes and grimaced until Sunny responded.

"Yeah, it was interesting. I usually put on music while I read, I found most of the songs too distracting for that." The list was twelve songs, and Gladson titled it, "For Sunny." None of the songs had true lyrics. Some had feminine focal noises. "What do you do while listening?"

"Do? You're so silly. I like to be still. Let the music sink into my brain."

He didn't say it, but Sunny pictured him sitting on his couch, in the dark, with headphones, smiling and nodding to the nightmare fuel he called music.

"Oh yeah, that makes sense."

Chapter 9

Current Day

THE OFFICE CHAIR OFFERED zero lumbar support. The wobbling armrests click-clacked when she moved. The hydraulic seal leaked. Bone connectivity is more real with age. Ryker gets heel pain if she stands too long. Glute pain if she sits too long. Her plantar-fasciitis-friendly tennis shoes tapped the carpet. She started this interview with a good three inches between her soles and the ground. *Fuck it, I'm already uncomfortable.* Ryker kicked off her shoes and hiked her feet into the chair. *Better.*

"Have you heard of second victim syndrome?" Felice asks.

"I'm the therapist now." Ryker hits her chest with an open hand.

Felice gave her an *are you finished* look.

"If it's okay with you," Ryker continued despite the judgmental glare. "I'd prefer to process this whole thing on my own. As you've established, we are not in a safe space."

"This was not the point you decided to call me."

"How are you sitting so straight? It's unnatural."

No response.

"Sorry, that was supposed to be an inside thought. Anywho." Ryker lifts her arms overhead. The tension in her shoulders releases along with a cat-like moan. "Did you ask me a question?"

"I did not. I was ensuring my timeline was correct."

"That's step three!" Ryker tries another high-five.

Felice keeps her forearms on the table.

"You're right. That's jumping too far ahead."

Thursday: Seven Days Ago

"BE NICE, SMILE, AND no one will accuse you of murder," Ryker said to her apartment. Prepping her vocals in the morning was a must before important communications. She made the mistake of calling the bank first thing one morning, and was immediately accused of accosting the customer service rep. *Remember, they can hear your smile.*

"Hi, this Ryker, I'm returning a call...Yes, I am on my way...I've been there before...Oh no, not for anything like this, I dropped my credit card and someone turned it in...Real good karma...Thanks."

She woke up to three voicemails. The first came at 0728, asking if Ryker could meet with a detective at 0900. The next at 0936, informing Ryker this was a serious matter and she was required to cooperate with Drivers police. The third, 1058, "I was just told by my uniformed officer you said you would be unavailable before 1100. Whenever you can come to the station is fine. Please call ahead so we know you're coming."

Showing up before a shift change meant zero parking. She zippered up and down each row until a woman in a printed scrub top, Karen haircut, and clutch of keychains flounced to a vehicle. One doesn't follow a Karen to her vehicle. The Karen will undoubtedly take fifteen minutes to leave if she knows you're waiting for her.

Instead of driving at her heels, Ryker pretended like she was leaving the lot. Karen took a minute, then backed out of the space. Ryker made a two-point turnaround at the gate and secured her spot. As she gathered her lunchbox and work bag from the passenger seat, Karen pulled up behind her.

"I'm just going to lunch. I still need to park here." She pointed as she spoke, rattling the ice in her tumbler.

Ryker didn't respond. This woman had no intention of allowing Ryker this beloved space. Not her fucking parking lot.

"Did you hear me? I'll be back in like ten minutes," she said through smacked gum.

Again, this did not warrant a response. The police station was across the street from the employee entrance, adjacent to the general lab. Walking at a brisk, but not hurried pace, Ryker cut through the drainage ditches and rocks that prevented the lot from turning into a lake when it rains.

Karen continued following Ryker, flailing her hand around. Probably similar to what she uses on her dogs and children, portrayed via vinyl decals on the rear window. Ryker was neither of those.

Caffeine is a prerequisite for life. Until her adenosine receptors were blocked and her brain was filled with sweet neurotransmitters, Ryker did not give a shit. The black SUV and entitled stranger weren't any kind of threat. Plus, she had bigger fish to stake.

Hell, hit me. A staycation sounds nice.

To Ryker's surprise, the woman followed her all the way to the police station. Inside, a man sat at a raised reception desk. A string of gold, red, and green fall leaves hung under the counter. Glittered pinecones adorned the ends and between each leaf. This was handmade and spectacular. He held a manicured finger up as Ryker entered. She offered a soft smile and stood in silence.

"Excuse me." Karen burst through the door. "You stole my parking spot, and you're trying to report me?"

Ryker made eye contact with the receptionist, who was still on his phone call.

"Hey, I'm talking to you." Karen grabbed Ryker's arm.

"Ma'am. No Ma'am. No. Ma'am." The receptionist shouted as he snapped his fingers. "I'm gonna have to call you back." He put the phone down instead of hanging it up. "Get your hand off her."

Ryker stood, furious, her bicep in this stranger's grasp. "You will let go of me."

"Did you hear that?" Karen dropped Ryker's arm and cowered towards the chairs lining the glass front window. "She just threatened me."

"Ma'am, I'm going to need you to get in that chair." The receptionist motioned for Ryker to come to his desk. "Are you okay?"

"I'm pretty pissed she grabbed me. My name is Ryker. I was the one who found..."

The receptionist held his hand up. The rose polish sparkled in the light. "Can I see your employee ID?" He started typing, "And this," he said while waving his hand at Karen, "I saw the whole thing. I can make the report for you."

"That would be great. Thank you."

"You need a bottle of water or anything?"

"A cup of coffee would be nice." Last night, Ryker took a deep internet dive on the marks she saw on Eva's neck. Before she knew it, the sun was rising.

"I got you. Black?"

"Yeah."

"Sugar?"

"If it needs it."

"I'd love a bottle of water," Karen shouted. Technically, she was still in her seat. Like a child in timeout, she inched her body as far as possible off the chair while maintaining some semblance of contact.

"Ma'am, I am with another person. This is not your moment."

The door to the police station opened, a guy entered wearing cargo pants and a black collared shirt. Gun holstered to his thigh and a police badge hooked into his belt loop.

Karen fully popped out of her chair.

"Ma'am, if I have to ask you to sit one more time, I will be asking with a uniformed officer in here. Do you understand?"

The cop put one hand on his holster. Karen sat down, folding her arms across her chest.

"Ryker? Come with me." He nodded to the receptionist. The receptionist nodded back, waved the cop away, and pressed a button on his desk to unlock the door.

The decorations around the inside of the station were more appropriate for a kindergarten class than a crime prevention hub. Dozens of flavors of paper plate pies surrounded the main window. If they were having a decorating contest, reception had it in the bag.

"Thank you for coming in. I want to apologize in person for the early phone calls."

Ryker accepted the apology with a subtle nod as she sat at his desk.

"I'm Detective Russell. I'm running this investigation. First," he checked his notes, "We need to clarify the extent to which you touched Ms. Deluka."

"Who's Ms. Deluka?" Ryker scanned her memory. *Oh no, you answered a question with a question. Quick, say more words.* "Not that I have a habit of touching strangers." *Well fuck.*

"The woman whose body you found. Eva, the FDA inspector. The notes from the officer at the scene say you kicked her? Can you demonstrate how hard?"

"Oh, right. The one, single person I tippy tapped with my foot yesterday." Adjusting her chair for the correct angle, she lifted her foot, paused to aim, then jabbed the detective in his shin with her toes.

"For future reference, the floor or table leg would have been acceptable." He dusted off his pants. "Don't worry, I won't press charges this time."

"Sorry about that," she said, not meaning it. He should have been more specific.

"At any point did you see Elyssa Suarez enter the bathroom?"

"Elyssa? No. I saw Eva go in. There's no way Elyssa did this. She doesn't have enough weight on her to lower the lab chairs."

"I believe you, and Elyssa, just confirming everyone's story. Did you see anyone other than Eva Deluka go into the bathroom?"

"Like that day? Or around the time of the murder?" *Do they think someone went into the bathroom and waited in the stall for the kill?*

"We haven't concluded this was murder. Was there anyone else in the bathroom with Eva?"

"Other than me?" *How could they not call this a murder?*

"You said you didn't follow her in."

"I didn't." *Did they know this was a supernatural crime and are trying to cover it up? Do they work for the SSB?*

"So how were you in the bathroom with her?"

"That's how I found her body."

"While Eva was alive, did you see anyone in the bathroom with her?"

"I didn't see Eva alive in the bathroom."

"I need you to answer yes or no."

"Okay."

"Listen," Detective Russell sighed. "I understand finding a dead body can be stressful." He placed his hand on Ryker's shoulder, "For the next series of questions, will you please respond with a yes or no?"

"Can do." She meant it as a joke, but his silence indicated the questions had already started. "Yes, yes, I can."

Detective Russell went through the names of everyone in the blood bank that day. Ryker admitted to not seeing any of them in the women's bathroom with Eva. Before going through a second list of names, Russell prefaced it by saying these people worked in Pharmacy. They share the breakroom across from the bathroom, it's possible one of them was around during the time of death.

"One final thing. Can you think of anyone who would want to hurt you?"

Ryker wasn't prepared for this question. The truth slipped out before she could consider the consequences. "There's one in your waiting room."

Detective Russell leaned in, "Yesterday, did you do anything to offend anyone or make them angry?"

"Probably."

"Have you noticed anything out of the ordinary happening? Any abnormal behavior towards you?"

"Every interaction I have with someone on first shift is abnormal. Have you tried having a conversation with any of them?"

"Humor me. Give an example," his pencil at the ready.

"Malia does turnover with the space above my shoulder, in as few words as possible. Liam fucking stares at me wide-eyed all the time. Quinneth has been sabotaging me all week. I'd say she's doing it on purpose, but she's not good enough at blood banking to know how to set someone up. Let's not forget Dr. Kudela. Dude sticks his tongue out of his mouth whenever I talk, it's weird as shit. Wait. Do you think I was the intended target?"

"No, no, nothing like that. Well, not exactly. Officer Whyte made several notes of your coworkers comparing Eva to you. Including the physical similarities from the back." He gave Ryker the once-over.

"We have the same butt?" she asked, perplexed.

"Hairstyle."

"No. That makes less sense. Do you know how many people wear their hair in a bun? Unless you think this guy has some kind of kink."

"Not only are you assuming murder. You're assuming it's a man?"

"Yes."

"Until the medical examiner makes her decision, we're investigating all possibilities. Tell me more about Quinneth. You said sabotage."

"I also said there's no way she's smart enough to do it on purpose." *She can't be a vampire. They have to be smart, right? They live so long.* "Contaminating the Duffy antisera, the fucking screening cells, not to mention the irradiation requirement. Quinneth is the whole reason Eva showed up in the first place. No way she planned all of that. She can't plan a rule-out panel."

"Would it be possible for you to refrain from swearing during our interview. Who's Duffy?"

"Not if you want me to be honest. Duffy isn't a person. They may have been at one point. I don't remember what the system is named after. Duffy antisera. It's a monoclonal anti-Duffy B reagent. It's something we use for testing."

"You said, mono..."

"It's not worth repeating." Another automatic response. It didn't land well.

"Excuse me?"

"If one of my coworkers had the tits to kill me, they wouldn't do it at work."

"How would you, they, do it, then?"

"They'd get my address from the mass casualty roster. Follow me to the park I hike in every Saturday. Chloroform me in the woods, inject me with phenobarbital, and toss me in the river. No body. No Crime."

"Until you decompose and your body floats to the surface."

"Not if they cut my stomach open and rip apart my intestines first." Ryker shook her head. No way he worked for the SSB. This man could use a couple hours of TikTok homework on how to hide a body. "Killing me is a dead end. What about the marks on her neck?"

Who would want me dead enough to commit homicide but be so bad at murder they accidentally kill Eva? Maybe it was Quinneth.

"Strangulation marks? My officer didn't note any?"

"No, they were more like hole punches. Or a big ass spider bite."

"We should be on the lookout for a gigantic male spider? How about you leave the investigation up to the police?" he smirked. "If I need my blood drawn, I'll let you know."

I'm not a phlebotomist.

His face annoyed Ryker on multiple levels. How do you explain to someone they insulted you wrong? Russell leaned back in his chair, no doubt waiting for Ryker to respond. She reached for her cup of coffee, but it was empty. Hands in motion, she placed them under her legs and let out an automatic yawn. "My shift is about to start. Do I need to check out with the clerk?"

Russell's eyes darted to her thighs. Ryker immediately brought her hands in front of her and cracked her knuckles. More of an anxiety relief than a threat.

"Here, take this," he plucked a business card from a golden Pi card holder and wrote on the back. "Have your boss call me if you're late. We can't have you punished for assisting in an investigation." His fingers touched hers as she reluctantly accepted the card.

The detective escorted Ryker to the waiting area. His hand brushed against the small of her back, leading her through the doorway. He dropped it when he caught the daggers coming out of the receptionist's eyes. After Ryker cleared the door, Detective Russell called the woman from the parking lot. Her real name was Tammy. Through sobs, she protested her innocence.

I should've been nicer.

All you did was park your car. She made her own choices.

"Thank you for the coffee," Ryker said as she passed the receptionist.

"Have a nice day," he said with a big grin and pointed to the window.

Another choice Tammy made was to park in a police spot in front of the station. A tow truck locked onto the vehicle as Ryker crossed the street to the employee entrance. If Tammy hadn't stalked Ryker to the police station, would anyone have given a shit? Had she tailgated Ryker out of the parking lot, yelling obscenities, then driven off, how big of a pain would it have been to report her?

Would they think I deserved it?

Chapter 10

Current Day

EYES FOCUSED, HANDS AND feet still, Felice's stamina is exquisite.

"Can I get a coffee? And a snack?" Ryker allows her head to fall back as she lets out a yawn. "To answer your question, I did not know he left."

Felice knocks on the door and whispers to the guard outside.

"Regina said Desmund mentioned demons, that didn't raise any red flags?"

"Eventually." Ryker wiggles in her chair, summoning the energy to continue.

"Did you follow up on the crystals noted when he first arrived?"

"Did I look in his chart? Without a blood order? That's a HIPAA violation," Ryker says, adding some thickness to her twang.

"You ate potato chips in the lab. That's an OSHA violation."

"Yes, but in that scenario, I thought we were all going to die anyway. I took a risk with my personal safety. That is very different than breaking the rules to risk someone else's safety. Moreover," she took a deep breath to prepare for the speech that has been in her head for a long time. "Techs are not responsible for direct patient care. We are not in the room with patients. Knowing what organs critical chemistry results impact does not make you a doctor. Patients do not consent to techs perusing through their charts, scoffing at the tests their provider ordered. People aren't lab values. Techs have no right to scroll through Emergency Department notes for interesting backstories. Telling me to get ready because the trauma in room four has a low hemoglobin does nothing. If I don't have a type and screen, if I don't have a blood order, there is nothing to get ready. If techs cared about patients, they would respect their right to privacy."

"After you met with Detective Russell, that's when you decided to investigate Eva's murder?" Felice asks.

"Yes, but not, like, right after."

Thursday: Seven Days Ago

Fifteen minutes left before her shift started. Ryker considered going to the new Malaky's coffee in the main gift shop. The twitch in her left eye told her she reached her daily caffeine threshold. Opting out of coffee gave her a few minutes in the breakroom with her current ebook. *Yes, follow the creepy puppet into the hidden basement.*

"Ryker. Good. Did I startle you? What time does your shift start? Soon? Stop by my office before you put on your coat." Fatima spoke too quickly for Ryker to answer. She swooped in, rinsed out her food container, dried it with a paper towel, and left.

1439, Ryker continued reading. Sort of. Every pause in the story, every comma or period, her mind drifted off. *What did I do this time?* Parking Lot Tammy pushed the limit of Ryker's willingness to get yelled at. Sure, you got yelled at in the Navy. You also got to yell back. Not to everyone. Throw a temper tantrum back into someone's face one or two ranks above you, you didn't always get an ass chewing. Sometimes the whole department got lectured on respectful communication. No one took volume personally. Tone wasn't a qualifier for disrespect, especially if your uniform was crisp.

Stacks of papers covered Fatima's desk and teetered on a chair in the corner of her office. Reference books and binders scattered throughout the bookcase behind her desk. One of the binders read, "Mass Casualty Plan." *That's where that went. Good thing that hasn't come up.*

"Ryker, I want to ask you about the screen cells yesterday." Fatima tapped the incident report in front of her. "Can you explain why you QC'd a new lot?"

"Per my report, the new lot was placed on the instrument. I thought that was a mistake. When I went to the back, the old lot appeared to be exhausted. I QC'd the new lot to continue patient testing." I statements were key. Avoid blaming words.

"I checked the timeline on the machine, you were the one logged in when the new lot went on."

"Correct. I checked that as well. However, I was not the person who loaded those reagents. Anyone can walk up and load things on the machine."

"Why didn't you take those off and replace them with our current lot?"

"Like I reported, there weren't any sets of the current lot remaining."

"Then why did Malia find seventeen boxes in the storage room?" Fatima pulled out an empty screen cell box.

"What the hell?" A surge of anger rushed through her body.

"Ryker, please, answer my question."

"I don't know where Malia found those. The only lot in the reagent fridge was the new lot."

"You didn't look in any other fridge?"

"They aren't stored in any other fridge."

"How am I supposed to help you become a better tech, Ryker, if you refuse to take accountability?" Fatima asked.

Anxiety and anger took over Ryker's body. She wasn't allowed to make mistakes. Other techs, June, Elyssa, if they made a mistake, it was no big deal. Easy fix. We can move on. Ryker held herself to a higher standard, and it appears Fatima did, too.

"Ryker, I need an answer, Ryker. Do you take responsibility for your actions or no?"

That was a bullshit question. Ryker knew she didn't load those reagents. She knew where the current lot was supposed to be stored. She knew she didn't contaminate that antisera. She knew if she'd issued that exchange the exact way first shift left it for her, Fatima would've told her she should have known better.

"I do take accountability for my actions. That's why I hold my peers responsible for the same level of accuracy in their work as myself. If those reagents weren't stored in the proper fridge. Then, yes, I missed them. All the work I reported yesterday was with QC'd reagents. Yes, it's best practice to use an entire lot before switching to a new one, but it isn't FDA reportable. It isn't against CLIA, CAP, or AABB guidelines. Someone, who wasn't me, loaded that lot before it was QC'd and tried to use it for patient testing. That is an incident report."

She didn't ask for permission to leave. It was get out now or sling four-letter words at a supervisor. Job hunting between November and January required patience and a ton of savings. Ryker had her rainy-day fund. If she didn't cash it in after the outbreak, she wasn't going to let some quality assurance supervisor run her off. Fatima thinks Quinneth is a good tech. That tells Ryker all she needs to know regarding the value of Fatima's approval.

Desk was abandoned by the time Ryker returned. Her hand shook as she logged into her workstation. The fear of getting in trouble for standing up for herself began to outweigh her sense of self-respect. Boundaries and emotional maturity are irrelevant when you engage with someone who isn't operating in good faith. Fatima had no intention of hearing out Ryker's side. The constant use of her name made Ryker want to hit her over the head with a folding chair.

Inhale four seconds, hold it, exhale four seconds. Routine dictated Ryker check her emails before engaging in bench work. The first was from Drivers. A reminder for the upcoming Thanksgiving Memorial Dinner and Hero Celebration. One plate of food per person. Turkey, mashed potatoes, stuffing, optional gravy. A vegetable lasagna would be provided as a vegetarian option. Everyone is welcome to a drink of their choice from the drink fountain. Dessert will be either pecan or sweet potato pie.

The second email was from Liam, with a reply from Dr. Sanders. The blood bank passed the surprise inspection. Dr. Sanders would like to celebrate by buying everyone pizza on Friday.

The third, also from Liam, to both the blood bank and pharmacy. An earring was found by environmental staff in the women's bathroom. If anyone has lost one, please share its description in an emailed response to Liam.

"Transfusion, this is Ryker...No, I just got here, we did shift change, how can I help you...Let me take a look, can I have the patient's medical record number...Yes, I see your plasma order...Oh, you are correct, we do not triage orders from labor and delivery, yes, that is ready right now."

Every fucking day with Quinneth. Ryker also kicked herself for saying the FFP was ready without checking the fridge for which types were thawed. There should be five group As at all times. The patient was group O, should be fine. Things have not been going as they should when she follows Quinneth. Seven As, three Os, and two ABs. Plenty.

"Transfusion, this is Ryker. How can I help you...Yes, we canceled that as a duplicate...We can't do another type and screen today...We did one yesterday and the patient has not been discharged...Yes the screen was positive yesterday...Even if we ran another screen today and it was negative, we would continue providing antigen negative blood and serological crossmatches...Yes, even if the screen was negative for the rest of the patient's life, we would still provide antigen negative blood and serological crossmatches...That's how the immune system works...Our on call resident can provide you with more information...Thank you."

An hour and a half before lunch. Liam and Dr. Sanders were in Liam's office with the door open so she couldn't play her New York Times games. Not without risking either of them sneaking up on her. It would be a cold day in the Texas summer before Ryker wished for work to do, but she was grateful for the distraction of a pickup request in the tube station. Except, this one had a pink top sample tucked into the papers. Sure enough, there was a red blood cell order and a type and screen pending for this patient.

Ryker time-stamped the pickup request, and received the sample. "STAT with a blood order and pickup from the ED."

"Did you call them to let them know the blood wasn't ready?" Elyssa asked as she read the orders.

"No, they should know it's not ready. They'll call if they can't figure it out."

"What was up with Fatima's attitude when she left?"

"She accused me of not looking for the rest of the reagents, so I accused her of killing Eva."

"Oh, shit." A big smile spread over Elyssa's face.

"Not really," Ryker sighed, "I walked out of her office before she dismissed me. She might have taken the murder accusation less personally."

"So are you putting together a list of suspects?" She took the sample out of the centrifuge.

"If I were investigating, I'd start with Fatima. Next is Liam, cause he's management and they're all evil. Draining the life out of us for a paycheck."

"Of course," Elyssa agreed.

"Then June, due to her wild card nature. Yvette, though I think she'd be most likely to get away with murder. Then there's you. You started here at a very suspicious time." Ryker turned and made eye contact as she spoke. It was meant to be a joke, a dramatic effect. Elyssa suddenly seemed nervous.

"You've narrowed it down to everyone who was in the lab except you." She moved out of Ryker's eyesight. "What would be Fatima's motive?"

"Maybe Eva discovered Fatima's deep, dark secret? Fatima was hired to hide blood bank mistakes. Eva saw right through her."

"Hide mistakes by blaming them on you? That's a bit of a stretch."

"It's a working theory." Ryker said, knowing her accusation lacked facts, or logic.

"Not to be insensitive, but it seems like you're taking Eva's death personally," Elyssa said.

"I know Drivers is going to fuck this up. A meets expectations investigation. Just like they did after the outbreak. I know for a fact one patient died of a transfusion reaction, but they called the cause of death combustion."

"What do you mean?"

"The tech of the quarter claimed the patient's plasma was too icteric. Said he got the reverse B cells confused with the anti-B antisera. He typed them as B pos instead of O pos. Then he said he had so many confirm types that day, he did the second type on the same sample by mistake. We issued B pos. The floor gave it. The patient exploded."

"Do they still work here?"

Tinkslllptink. Ryker's lanyard hit the floor between her legs. Sigh.

"I put a wrench through his head. He was already dead when I did it. Unlike Eva, who was alive and well when Fatima sucked the life from her." She re-hooked the clasp and placed it around her neck.

"I can tell you it wasn't Fatima." Elyssa stifled her laugh.

"She left during the time of death."

"No, she didn't. Not to trigger any screen cell issues, but I think you just didn't see her. I heard her *good evening, everyone*, right before you came in and told us you found the inspector. I don't know how long it takes to suck the life out of a person. Fatima has never moved that fast."

"Hmmm," Ryker grunted.

The timestamp on the counter sounded. The request said FFP. Elyssa made a bag of ice while Ryker issued the products.

If Elyssa was correct about the timeline, then fine, Fatima didn't kill Eva. Someone in the lab was definitely setting Ryker up to fail. At least, they were trying. Maybe it wasn't enough that she got yelled at. Maybe they were pissed she thwarted their efforts more than once. Were the two connected? Detective Russel thought they were. That was enough for Ryker to know they weren't.

A STAT order printed for a unit of blood. The patient had a previous Anti-E and Anti-K. The ER wanted the blood irradiated. Per their new policy, Ryker paged Dr. Kudela.

"Transfusion, this is Ryker...Yes, we received the order...Sorry, I meant I have the order, the blood is not ready...We don't have a type and screen, and the patient has a history of antibodies...If you need blood right now, it would have to be uncrossmatched...Thanks."

Before she hung up the phone, the printer shot off the uncross-matched order. Patient was male, so technically, Ryker could issue any O pos unit. Until she got the pickup request, she had time to search for already tested antigen-negative units. *Shit.* The dedicated shelf didn't have any that were E and K negative. Time to steal.

A blood bank hack Ryker learned from her third shift trainer when she started at Drivers, if it's not on the available shelf, try the crossmatched shelf. Those units can be replaced, there is no undo button for an acute hemolytic transfusion reaction. Perfect. The STAT RBCX had a unit left over, C, E, and K negative. Plus, it was irradiated. If the requirement was later approved by Dr. Kudela, it would mean bonus points to Ryker.

The time stamp sounded.

"I'm here for the uncrossed blood for E-4," she handed Ryker a patient chart sticker.

Ryker handed it back to her, along with a blank pickup request card. "Place the sticker on the card, write what you're picking up here, write the provider's name here, and your employee number here."

While the nurse followed orders, Ryker released the unit from its previous owner and pulled a segment for crossmatching later. Ryker took the card from the nurse who nailed Ryker's instructions.

"I wanted to bring the paper like normal, but everyone said to bring a sticker for uncrossed blood." The nurse tapped her fingers on the counter.

"The paper would have been perfect. Would have saved you from having to fill out the card." Ryker spoke as she scanned the unit for issue.

"I knew I was right. I'll tell them downstairs." The nurse took the card back from Ryker to perform the blood product readback; name, medical record number, date of birth, quantity, and type of requested products.

When the nurse left, Ryker opened the SAGA chart of the patient whose blood she stole. Nice, they were discharged. The unit wouldn't need to be replaced.

"Transfusion, this is Ryker…Irradiation indicated, okay, well, they ordered uncrossmatched, so I gave them irradiated just in case…Thanks."

The pager sounded. "Level 1 trauma, male, 25 years old, multiple wounds, possible animal attack, ETA five minutes.

"Guys, guys, my kids just sent me a video." June rushed to the front of the lab. "This lady found someone in the Drivers parking lot. She said it looked like he had a hospital gown, but it was torn to shreds. She recognized the bright green patient arm band and called 911."

An order for two units of uncrossmatched low-titer group O Whole Blood printed. Patient name Delta, J. In the order comments, the doctor added a presumed name, "Desmund Nwadike."

Chapter 11

ON THE LAST DAY of her first week, Gladson signed Sunny's competency packet.

"Congratulations! You're competent in specimen receiving and processing."

This week, she was moving on to testing and Nevasha. Fingers crossed, she was finally getting to the good stuff.

"Before we get started, I want to go over last week with sample processing."

Sunny's heart dropped.

"How fucking creepy is Gladson? Did he send you that playlist?"

Clarification, comfort, and recognition all in one sentence. "Oh my god, yes. And yes."

"He sends that playlist to almost every woman who trains here. He named it *For Sunny*, right? It's like he has a playlist of moves to hit on women at work. I complained about him and how close he sits while you're trying to log in samples. He says it's welcoming, and blames the screen filters for needing to sit so close."

"Oh my god, did he get in trouble?"

"No." Nevasha rolled her eyes. "He was told not to use the work phone list to send non-work-related text messages. That was only after I fought to get him to admit I did not give him permission to text me socially. You didn't get any texts from him, did you?"

"No. That would have made me super uncomfortable. I'm sorry you had to go through all that."

"I'm sorry for all the women who went through it before me. Shit, he's coming back here." Nevasha logged into her computer.

"So I know it's a bit unexpected, but we were talking about recipes so much it got me in the mood for baking. Not to toot my own horn, but I made the best batch of carrot cake this weekend." He mimed drooling.

"Good for you." Sunny nodded.

"I'd love for you to try it, it's in the breakroom."

"She's allergic to gluten." Nevasha blurted out before Sunny could respond.

"Yeah, I am, sorry."

"You don't need to apologize for having allergies. It's not like he made the entire cake just for you. I'm sure Winston and Trevor will enjoy having it, again."

"It's strange how many people in this lab have Celiac disease." His face went cold.

"Don't you mean how many women in the lab?" She emphasized the word women. Without a goodbye, a smirk, or any gesture indicating he remembered Sunny was standing there, Gladson walked away.

Sunny waited until he sat down at the front desk, "Thanks for stepping in with the allergy thing. I didn't know what to say. I do not want to eat that cake. He looked really upset."

"He does it every fucking Monday after he trains. Don't feel bad, the guys know the drill. Trevor says he needs to work on his sugar ratio and stop lining the pan with coconut oil, but they'll gladly eat all of it before lunch. Apparently, most of his stuff isn't too bad dipped in coffee. They take turns bringing in extra cream cheese frosting."

"This might sound prickly." Sunny hesitated.

"Please continue."

"It's so nice to hear you say you don't like Gladson. Even nicer to hear sarcasm and snarkiness at work."

"Oh my god. Did Felice send you to St. Mary's? She sent me there, too! It's a fucking game for her. She sends us to labs that make us uncomfortable. It's one of the many ways she assesses us. Cool people go to St. Mary's. Gladsons go to the VA. I got fired within two weeks. How long did you last?"

"Three god damn months! Are you saying if I got fired, I could've started training here sooner?"

All the times Sunny bit her tongue. The phone calls she forced herself to smile through. The apologies she made when nurses did things wrong. People pleasing torture.

"Wow. The force is strong with this one. Don't worry, you're here now, god dammit." She patted Sunny on the shoulder. "Let's focus on that. This is hematology."

Nevasha explained they'd begin by reviewing normal slides. Performing manual white blood cell differentials and noting red blood cell morphology. Once Sunny got the hang of a normal diff, they'd get into more complicated slides.

It had been a while since she performed a diff. She was nervous about confusing reactive lymphocytes for monocytes or missing inclusions. Her worst fear, she'd say she was done, then realize she'd forgotten to examine the red cells.

Her first count took twenty minutes to reach one hundred white cells. Not because of difficulty. Sunny took the time to double-check a few cells against her chart. Anytime she changed cell types, she had to lift her head to verify she pressed the correct button on her diff counter. Diff counters are similar to calculators. Each number/button is labeled with the type of white cell it represents: basophils, eosinophils, monocytes, lymphocytes, band neutrophils, segmented neutrophils, and "blank" buttons to be set by the lab. It took a couple refresher slides to relax. Soon, she was breezing through and pressing the buttons on her diff counter without moving her eyes from the microscope.

The next slide was different. "Wow," Sunny bit her inner cheek. "All of these red cells are nucleated and elliptical. I've never seen anything like this."

"Good," Nevasha clapped. "That's bird blood. You noticed the blazing obvious. Reptiles and fish also have nucleated red blood cells. Go ahead and find a neutrophil for me."

Sunny turned the stage controls until she was centered on a bright pink, granulated cell.

"Great," Nevasha said. "That's an eosinophil. Birds don't have neutrophils, they have heterophils. The difference is more than just nomenclature. That's part of training. I told you all that to say it can be difficult, at first, to tell the difference, so don't be distraught. Today is more about exposure to the differences. Later, we'll worry about getting everything correct. Honestly, unless you were a vet or something, it would be really weird for you to know all this."

"So I'm going to learn veterinary differentials in a week?" Sunny asked, terrified at the prospect.

"What? No. Sorry. I skipped that part." Nevasha flipped the pages on a packet of papers Sunny hadn't noticed before. "It's the first thing I was supposed to tell you, and I always miss it because it's bold and highlighted." Nevasha cleared her throat. "We do week-long introductory training in each department. After you've experienced the departments we want to show you, you'll be assigned to either a home base department or as a field agent."

"Oh, that's nice. Why didn't Gladson tell me that?"

"Other than being a total nob gobbler? That one is on the SSB. The longer you stay, the more information they trust you with."

"Like last names?" Sunny asked.

"Those are on the do not reveal list. The less we know about each other, the less likely we are to associate with each other outside of work, according to some weird study. The less we care about our coworkers, the less we care about their work. Social and informational compartmentalization.

"If the agency ever decides to kill me, no one will report me missing because I never existed to them."

"Now she gets it." Nevasha shot finger guns. "Take a look at this one and tell me what you notice." She pulled another slide out of a cardboard slide tray labeled *Week 1*.

Sunny's hematology instructor was very strict about slide and microscope etiquette. She worked with some techs who would drag out the old slide and shove the next one into the stage clip. Like nails on a chalkboard. Sunny turned the objective, lowered the stage with the coarse adjustment, and looked at something in the distance to relieve eye strain. She got her new slide, found her starting field under 40x, added a dollop of oil to her slide, and turned to the 100x objective. Now she was ready for her standard diff count pattern. Down, right, up, right, down, right, up, right. Making a boxy zigzag as she panned across the slide.

"I see lots of rouleaux, and it's hard to tell with them all stuck together, but the red cells are tiny." Sunny kept scanning, "Oh. Is this an eosinophil? It looks like it's made of styrofoam."

"Styrofoam! That's a great description. I always say pastel baked beans." After peeking through the eyepiece, "Yes. That's it. This is horse blood."

"Wait." A lightbulb went off in Sunny's head, "Do centaurs have human eosinophils and styrofoam ones?"

"Fuck yes." Nevasha punched one hand in the air. "I cannot confirm or deny the existence of some woodland creatures who make for really fun Punnett squares. But I can tell you, keep that train of thought, not just in heme, in all the departments."

END OF SUNNY'S SECOND week. Now, when Sunny enters the lab, Gladson pretends to be busy on his computer. No hello's, no waves, not even a grin. Thank god. The idea that everything he said was part of a plan that ended with her enthralled by carrot cake was disturbing. The poor girl who falls for his shtick, would he actually care about her? Is the woman relevant? Is his only concern her ability to fit into his mold of a relationship? Gross.

"Last day. You've breezed through the basics, so I get to show you some of my favorite case studies. And. The best part. You've been cleared to know about our current SBOI, Supernatural Being of Interest. Let's look at the slide first. You tell me what you see, then take a guess."

Nevasha unlocked a filing cabinet with a key she wore on her One Piece lanyard. Instead of a slide folder, these were in a black box. An inventory sheet lined the lid. The slides stood on a dark wood base, and light wood slide spacers kept them evenly separated and secure.

"That's beautiful," Sunny said.

"Aww, thanks. I made it. I 3D printed the case. The bottom is mahogany, and the spacers are teak. Woodworking keeps me from running out and telling everyone all the agency's secrets. If I'm feeling particularly stressed, I can shout those thoughts while my saw is running. No one hears me, so I'm not breaking any rules, and the thought gets out of my head." She placed the case on the solid black lab countertop, "Go ahead and take out slide number five."

"Like butter," Sunny said.

"It took me hours of sanding. That little bit of friction on the glass when it hits a rough edge makes me shudder." Nevasha demonstrated a full-body shake. "Same thing as all week. White cells first, then red cell morphology and anything else you might see."

The way she said the last part, Sunny's heart raced. Part of her brain shouted at her, warning her not to mess this up. She told her brain, "Thank you for the concern, and please direct that energy into the diff."

"Oh, okay, well, there's lots going on with the red cells already. I see target cells, polychromasia, definite anisocytosis, schistocytes, let me count." At white cell three, she saw the inclusion. "Death Crystals."

"Bad ass. Not many techs have seen them before."

"Just once. She was an older woman with liver cirrhosis. She tried to quit drinking so she could watch her grandkids grow up. Every day, her lactic acid value increased. I saw the crystals one night while I was in heme. I didn't know what they were. Google said they meant imminent death. I wanted to call the nurse, call the doctor, so they could let her family know. My supervisor said that was beyond our scope. I sent the slide for the pathologist to review. She died the next morning. I think about her sometimes. Wonder if anyone got to say goodbye."

"Well, if it makes you feel any better, she might not be dead dead."

Sunny picked her head up from the microscope, "Are these zombie crystals?"

"Even better." Nevasha golf clapped. "Okay. I'm sure you read all the nonsense about scientists thinking these were made of bile. Then they examined one and it's lipid-based, not acid. Some people view these as a death calling card, others think it's overhyped. My sample size is low. But. Death Crystals have been found in every confirmed victim of a vampire bite.

"These are vampire crystals?"

"Yes. No. Maybe. That's the focus of my research. It would be, if Felice ever approves it. I think the crystals are more circumstantial. Something in the bites increase lactic acid levels in the human body. Possibly to help preserve it for transformation. Currently, she says there isn't enough evidence to warrant the exposure. We'd have to send a field agent to collect real-time data and interview potential vampire victims. She also says I get too emotional with vampire research. My mom was killed by one."

"Oh my god, I'm so sorry. That must have been horrifying." Sunny clutched her chest.

"It was a long time ago. I was eight. My mom got breast cancer. She had to have a double mastectomy." Nevasha told this story like she's told it dozens of times. "The next morning, we were visiting her in the hospital. She said she was cold and the blankets weren't keeping her warm, so my dad offered to get her a cup of coffee. My brother and I asked mom to play hide and seek with us. She kept her eyes closed and guessed where we were hiding. While we were under her bed, I heard the door open. I assumed it was dad, I thought I would jump out and scare him. My shirt got caught on something. Before I could jump out, I heard muffled screams and felt the bed shake.

"I heard a strange voice say, *Tell your kids to stay put, and they get to live.*

"Our mom's voice struggled, but she told us, *It's okay, babies, I love you, don't move until dad comes. He'll be back soon.*

"I watched him leave. I go to my mom. She has two little holes in the side of her neck. I'm shaking her, repeating, *mom, mom,* but she doesn't move. I run for help. I find my dad in the hallway talking to some nurses. By the time they got to my mom's room, she was dead. No one believed me. They said she had a stroke caused by the surgery."

There was nothing melodramatic about Nevasha as she retold her family tragedy. Instead, she opened a filing cabinet and revealed a tattered, dirty manila folder. "I told you all that to show you this. It's my mom's."

The ink on the handwritten chart was faded. The cursive might as well have been the Da Vinci Code. A clean, typed version of each page was filed adjacent to the original. Sunny skimmed through the lab results. The CBC and urine test looked like drug store receipts.

"I've asked multiple times if we could use Gladson to expand my research. We wouldn't have to send out a field agent. Felice won't force him to be part of an experiment. He's confirmed he can smell the crystals when they form. But he claims he isn't sure how or exactly when. He also won't spill the tea on how he became a vampire. It's so annoying."

"Slow down. Gladson is a vampire?" Sunny asked.

"Yeah, he's the only one on staff. At least, the only open one on staff. It used to be his pickup line. I guess he saves it to make him more mysterious."

Sunny could not wrap her head around Gladson being a supernatural creature. Vampires are cool. Sexy. Magnetic. Guess he got the repel end of the stick. "All that recipe talk?"

"Right? It's even creepier when you know he doesn't eat the food. He wants to feed you so he can smell it in your blood."

"That's so..."

"Creepy?" Nevasha asked.

"Boring. He's an immortal, I'm assuming vampires are immortal?"

Nevasha waved her hand, "Ageless, but can be killed, please continue."

"He has all this time to learn how to make delicious, fragrant foods: pizza, lumpia, curry, cinnamon rolls, brownies. Hell, zesty ranch crackers would be more interesting than carrot cake."

Chapter 12

Current Day

"**They pronounced him dead** a few minutes after giving him the whole blood. We never got a type and screen. That video June showed us was all over the news, with his name and photo." Ryker sips her coffee from a Dallas Zoo mug. She pulled from her memory, trying to determine if the mug came from the breakroom.

"How did Drivers respond to the report?" Felice taps at the groove between her nose and left cheek. Her first sign of fatigue.

"Not well," Ryker says. "They blamed Desmund for leaving AMA. Then they tried claim the video wasn't taken in a Drivers parking lot, but the apartment complex across the street. He lived there."

"The manner of death was different from Eva's, and before sunset. Yet, you were adamant this was a second vampire victim. Why?"

"It was too suspicious that a guy who claimed a demon was after him died from an animal attack. Buffy says sunlight kills vampires.

Twilight says it makes them sparkle. I didn't have any reason to believe there couldn't be an in-between. As far as manner of death, they're vampires, not serial killers. I take that back. They are serial killers. They just lack a dramatic recipe."

"Did you have any suspects in mind?"

"At this point, everyone."

"Including yourself?"

"I read this book that was a cross between Swamp Thing and Dr. Jekyll and Mr. Hyde."

Felice unamused.

"I promise this ain't a dull stick."

Felice blinks.

"It's got a point." Ryker mimes a double snare drum hit with a cymbal crash.

Felice gives her nothing.

"Anywho. It didn't go into the exact science of how the monster formed. But I wasn't ruling out the possibility that I drank some weird wine from the gas station and developed a secret split personality that craves blood straight from the tap."

"Perhaps you should stop buying wine from a gas station," Felice says. Her words soft yet sharp.

"Are you kidding me? Where else am I going to get ready to eat taquitos, cheese dip, and a dusty box of sauvignon at 2347 on Tuesday? Speaking of, how's that snack coming?"

Friday: Six Days Ago

DONATIONS FLOODED INTO DRIVERS after the outbreak. Admin gave some bullshit legal reason the GoFundMe money couldn't go directly to the employees as the donors intended. Instead, they upgraded the gift shop to host Malaky's coffee. Hourly staff were generously allowed one free coffee each month. The coffee was a standard menu item, size small, non-transferable, and did not roll over to the next month if unused.

Black coffee, aka utility coffee, was for waking up. No fruity flavors, no syrups, no creamers. Utility coffee provided Ryker with the dark and bitter fuel her soul needed to face the day. Fancy coffee, lattes, macchiatos, cappuccinos, those were for emotional support. The barista greeted Ryker with a big, customer service smile, "Welcome to Malaky's, what can I get for you?"

Next to the cash register was a sign for a new drink, not listed on the menu. "Is that for real?" Ryker asked. An Everything but the Bagel Latte.

"It tastes better than you'd think. If you're into savory." The barista leaned forward to guide Ryker through the ingredients. "We line the cup with whipped cream, sprinkle in that Trader Joe's seasoning, then fill with your favorite flavor latte. You interested?"

"Can I get it as my freebie?" Ryker already knew the answer.

"Sorry, it's not available as a donor drink."

"No worries. I'll have an americano, please." Ryker unhooked her employee ID from around her neck.

"Room for cream?" The barista asked with much less enthusiasm.

"No thanks."

A white coat caught the corner of her eye. Ryker scuffed at how gross it was they let doctors wear their labcoats all over the place. Her look of cold disapproval changed to surprise when she realized who it was. Waiting at the pickup counter, Dr. Kudela, the tip of his tongue peeking out.

"Coffee makes the day better," Ryker said, hoping it resembled small talk. She would have been happy to ignore the man lizard, but his stare was too intense.

"Everything Mocha," the barista placed the cup between them while giving Ryker the side eye.

She really wanted me to order that weird ass coffee.

Kudela did not warm up to Ryker's feeble pleasantry. He left without saying anything in response. A few steps away from the counter, he hunched over. Coffee spewed onto the floor.

"Sir, are you okay?" The barista called out.

"Did you put garlic in this?" His hands dabbed at the leftover liquid on his mouth.

"I asked if you wanted the seasoning."

"I told you to leave out the garlic."

"I told you it comes in the seasoning."

"I'm allergic to garlic." Kudela's lips turned brighter with each sentence.

"Americano for Ryker," the barista called. "Do you want me to make you a different coffee? No charge."

"Can I get a plain mocha?" His face sagged with exhaustion, his eyes burned red.

1508, late but not too late. She had more tardy points to burn through than coffee filters. The nice thing about arriving late, most of first shift has already cleared the lab. She held her badge to the reader. Meep beep.

"Do you enjoy being this nasty of a person?" A tearful Quinneth raised her head from Fatima's embrace.

Confusion froze Ryker in her tracks. She envisioned herself signing in, glancing at the shift report, then going to Yvette's office with yesterday's free tardy note. Not walking into the worst tech ever, crying into the arms of the quality assurance supervisor.

"No?" Ryker waited for more words to come to her. They did not.

"Is this a joke to you? You think it's so funny to accuse me of murder?" Quinneth disembarked from the embrace and took a few steps towards Ryker.

Ryker let out an involuntary laugh. "I told them it couldn't be you."

"Then why did I spend the last two hours getting yelled at by him?"

Detective Russell offered a small wave. *Guess this tardy is officially going in the books.* She eased the card back into her pocket. Fatima escorted a still sobbing Quinneth out of the lab. *Coffee was a good call.*

"Now that all of second shift is here, Detective Robert would like to talk to you." If Liam knew what this was about, his face didn't give any indication.

"Hi, I am Detective Russell. I'll only take a few minutes of your time. I know you've got lots of blood donors waiting." He paused, as if he were expecting laughter or applause. Either this man has never donated blood, or detectives weren't taught context clues.

"Eva Deluka is a sheep farmer in Wyoming," another dramatic pause. Sheep farming is not the weirdest side gig a med tech has had. "That is to say, the woman who came to your lab on Wednesday is not Eva Deluka. We have renamed her Jane Doe. Other than the forged FDA badge, she didn't have any identification on her body. If any of you have any information as to her real identity, or find any of her belongings, please report them to Drivers PD."

June raised her hand.

"Yes, do you have information?" Detective Russell flipped open his notebook.

"Was Desmund Nwadike killed by the same person who killed fake Eva?"

Detective Russell closed his notebook. "Last night and this morning, a local news station incorrectly reported a Drivers patient was found dead on campus. An email today clarified the body was discovered near Drivers main campus. The person had been receiving treatment at Drivers but left against medical advice. That case is pending."

"Why did it take so long to figure out that wasn't her name? Don't you run fingerprints or background checks?" Yvette coming in hot.

"We are searching our available databases."

The women in the room gave each other disapproving glances.

"Fatima was the one who discovered the false identity," Liam said.

"Talk about quality assurance," Elyssa said.

Liam had a habit of freely sharing information. Knowing why they did things a certain way justified the emotional energy Ryker put into caring. Liam had a similar philosophy. It often led to him spilling more details than other managers might. It was one of the things Ryker liked most about him.

"She was submitting our corrective actions for the inspection. When she entered our case number, nothing pulled up on the website. Fatima called, thinking Eva was unable to submit our inspection before she passed. She wanted to submit both the report and the corrective actions. One supervisor led to another, and there was no record of an Eva Deluka working for the FDA." Liam paused for a breath, ignoring the you can stop there gesture from Detective Russell. "I googled Eva Deluka, and the only person I found was the sheep herder. I called Drivers PD. Detective Robert came, asked first shift if they had any information, then talked to Quinneth for a while." He raised his eyes and tilted his head towards Ryker during that last bit. "Now we're all on the same page."

"Again, my name is Detective Russell. I left my card with Liam," he said.

"It's on the board next to the bench rotation. Between the invitation to the Thanksgiving Memorial and Hero Dinner, and flu vaccine schedule. Oh, some unrelated news. Sunny informed me she has completed her time away. She will return to Drivers the first Monday in December. Was there anything else you needed, Detective?" Liam stood relaxed.

A tube crashed into the pile waiting to be unloaded from the station. It landed at an angle above the laser line. The "full" alarm sounded.

"That's it from me. I'll get out of your hair," he said, not moving.

Ryker wondered what hidden expectation they weren't meeting. How do other departments handle detectives? Cupcakes? Swooning?

"You ladies have a good evening. Be safe."

When the door shut behind the detective, Ryker let some non-caffeinated words slip out. "Fatima made more headway trying to submit a report than the actual police detective. How is this wank-stain going to solve a murder, two murders, when he can't solve the case of what a donor center is? Stay safe, my ass."

"By the way," A voice came from the service window. Detective Russell gave a cocky smirk, "If you ladies feel the need, any of my officers would be happy to escort you to your vehicles at night." He tapped the stainless steel counter with his notebook and continued down the hall.

A burst of smothered laughter filled the lab. Insulting people to their face required more nuance than insulting them behind their backs. Had Ryker remembered sound could travel into the hallway, she would have saved wank-stain for later.

The timestamp from the service window sounded. A nurse handed June a piece of paper.

"MTP in ICU," June announced as she searched through the stacks of pages on the printer to find the order. "A pos, no antibodies."

"Pizza will be here at 1700. I'll be in my office for a little while longer if you need me." Liam often offered help during MTPs on second shift. As a manager, he did not participate in the annual competency. Help from Liam would be making bags of ice, putting frozen products in to thaw, or clearing the tube station.

June sprinted for the ice machine. Some techs take the lead during a massive transfusion, others get ice. Ryker grabbed five A pos RBCs and the last five group A FFP and signed into the second desk computer. Manual work would have to wait.

"I need ten more group A plasma thawing," Ryker shouted as she scanned her units.

"I'm on plasma." Elyssa headed to the freezers.

Before Ryker packed the first shipment, a second runner showed up for shipment two.

June helped Ryker tag the units.

"This is Ryker in transfusion...We just gave out the first shipment, someone is here for shipment two. I won't have any plasma ready for fifteen minutes. Do you want them to wait for the plasma or take the cooler without it...Thanks." *Fuck.*

"Elyssa, start thawing the cryo for shipment three and five more A FFP."

Ryker grabbed another five A pos RBCs and a platelet. The ICU didn't want to wait for the FFP. The second cooler packed, ice provided by June, the second runner went on their way. By the time Ryker logged into her manual workstation, the plasma thawer alarmed, the units were ready. Elyssa was answering tests in automation, so Ryker went to the plasma.

Three of them had large, solid, frozen chunks. Ryker broke the chunks apart with her fingers and placed the units back in for a second round of thawing. The seven thawed units were modified in the LIS, five issued to the MTP.

"This is Ryker in transfusion, plasma is ready for shipment two...Thanks."

The first runner was back at the window before Ryker hung up the phone.

"They want the plasma and shipment three," June shouted on her way to get more ice.

Why didn't she start shipment three? Is she really not going to issue anything?

Again, Ryker went to the fridge for five units of A pos RBCs and the two ready plasma. Elyssa was at the plasma thawer waiting for the three units of FFP and the bag of pooled cryoprecipitate.

"Elyssa, I want to issue those with this, then we need five more plasma. Grab skinny units this time."

Skinny FFP is not a true scientific designation. It's what Ryker calls units less than 220 mLs. Less volume equals less thawing time. The thirty extra seconds taken to find skinny units are more than made up for by not having to do a bonus round of thawing.

Shipment three out the window. The bottom of the cooler was still visible when another runner handed Ryker her pickup card.

"This is Ryker in transfusion...We just sent shipment three...Yes, plus the missing FFP...Someone is here for shipment four and five...No, we will get one shipment ready at a time...Are you using the products...Okay, we're starting four now."

"What do you want us to do?" Yvette buttoned her labcoat. Liam was standing at her side.

"We need five more A plasma thawing. ICU agreed to send one runner for one shipment, but they said they would be sending a runner out as soon as one comes back. So far, they've transfused all products."

"I can do plasma," Liam said as he signed into the modifying workstation. "I'm not up to date on receiving samples, so I technically shouldn't do that."

"I'll stay up here and help June," Yvette directed. "You can go back to manual. There are a couple of samples that need crossmatches."

"Just reflexes left," Elyssa said from automated. "I did the STAT blood order. The antibody screen was negative today. It was easy."

Ryker let out a sigh of relief. It was so nice having a supervisor who took charge and a coworker with a similar work ethic. Everyone is capable of doing any of the work. If it's not assigned to you, but you have time, and the person it's assigned to is drowning, do the work. It almost felt like the old team was back together.

1718, the MTP was still active, but they were transferring the patient to the OR. The smell of wood-fired cheese and pepperoni filled the lab. Dr. Sanders always shelled out for good stuff. Yvette unlocked the empty office for pizza partying. Easy access to the food for blood bank, and less easy access for pharmacy. Pharmacy techs were ruthless after their cookie cake went missing.

"I know you're about to start break, is it okay if we talk for a second?" Yvette asked, reaching for a slice. "It won't count against your thirty minutes."

"Meetings with Ryker seem to be the hot new solution to everything," she said.

"As a friend, not a supervisor. Finding Eva is traumatic. I can tell you're taking her death personally. It's a terrible thing. Second victim syndrome is real. Considering the time of year. I wanted to check in. How's your head?"

"Still getting high fives afterwards."

Yvette's shoulders slumped. "Come on. You can talk to me. I messed up reporting that issue with June. You're last Thanksgiving..."

"Was last year. I'm fine. Other than Fatima blaming me for Quinneth's failures, I'm peachy."

"That's what I mean. I know you're a good tech. I believe you did what you thought was right."

"But you don't believe it was Quinneth?"

"The antisera, yes, but there was no patient harm. The screening cells, she probably loaded, but why would she hide the old lot number? People aren't going out of their way to make your day worse. No one is out to get you. Not here. I hate to say this, but you might be projecting your fears a little."

Tears formed behind her eyes. It's not fair that she cries when she suppresses her anger. Her body is fighting off the urge to rip the world to shreds, and it comes out as weak, salty droplets.

"I didn't mean to upset you," Yvette said.

"Someone killed Eva."

"They haven't ruled out natural causes."

"What if it were supernatural causes? I saw marks on her neck." Ryker said, giving Yvette a chance.

"I believe you. I need you to hear me when I say this, there can be marks on her neck, and she still died a natural death."

"You think Eva forged FDA credentials to sneak around our lab so she could have a stroke in the bathroom?" Ryker asked.

"It's the blood bank rule of threes. Once is a fluke, twice is a coincidence, three times is a pattern."

"If the parking lot attack was number two, who gets to be lucky number three?"

"Enjoy your pizza, you earned it." Yvette left.

Fueled by garlic sauce, pepperoni, diet Dr. Pepper, and spite, Ryker re-watched the news report about Desmund Nwadike. His sister said he texted her all day. He didn't feel safe at Drivers. She couldn't make it there until after dark. When she got to his room, he was gone. She drove to his apartment across the street, but he wasn't there either. His location share was on. She followed it to the Drivers employee parking lot. His body lay in the last drainage ditch. What was left of it. She didn't recognize him until she read the name on his bracelet.

There's no way this was a coincidence. Ryker knew who to call. She wasn't sure if she would pick up.

First ring, "Yes." The voice calm but assertive.

"This is Ryker Graden. You gave me your card."

"Don't waste time telling me things we both know."

"Drivers had an FDA inspection on Wednesday, the inspector was murdered. Last night, a patient left AMA. They found his body this morning.

"Sounds like the police have their hands full."

"Except the first victim didn't actually work for the FDA. They have no idea who she was and," Ryker hesitated. "They were killed by the same thing."

"Sounds like the FBI has their hands full."

"It was a vampire."

Long pause. Ryker checked the phone twice to ensure the call was still connected.

Felice burst into laughter. "Is this your big plan to join my agency? Make up a story about vampire murders? From what I hear, you can't identify an Anti-N antibody, and you think you can solve a double homicide? Who told you vampires existed? Buffy?" The line cut out.

Ryker knew why the SSB called Sunny first. Not many people like to give you opportunities after you call them an asshat. Prior to this phone call, she thought Sunny would get trained, come back to Drivers, and put in a good word for her. A better word than asshat.

Fuck it. Fuck Felice. Fuck the SSB. Fuck Drivers Police. These victims deserve justice. At least one of them definitely deserves justice. Eva may or may not have had it coming. If no one is going to take this seriously, then I'll solve it myself. Before anyone else gets killed.

Chapter 13

Current Day

"I DO NOT CACKLE like a hyena." Felice removes her glasses and cleans them with a cloth. Sign number two.

"I agree. Your laughter is rich and intelligent. I wanted to capture the menace. I wanted you to experience the level of anger I felt in the moment." Ryker repeats the laugh.

Felice folds the cloth and tucks it into her pocket.

Saturday: Five Days Ago

FRIDAY'S MTP LASTED UNTIL shipment eight. The pace only slowed down while they transferred the patient. Hospitals don't like patients dying in the Operating Rooms. If they can, they send them to the ICU for their final moments. Keeps the OR's numbers in the positive.

The first beer was to slow her adrenaline. Her body was still in fight mode. Even after Yvette took over as MTP commander, it remained an all-hands-on-deck scenario. Between the phone calls from the OR, the multiple calls from Dr. Kudela wanting to add irradiation requirements, and the nonstop specimens coming through the tube station, Ryker didn't have time for the Wordle or Connections, much less to plan a murder investigation. The second beer was to stop her from thinking about the phone call with the anesthesiologist. No other department in the hospital was expected to pump out product like the blood bank. Because the first two beers worked so well, she reached for a third and a snack.

Last Night Ryker set her alarm, determined to start her day early and strong. Six-mile walk first thing in the morning. Get ready for work. Visit victim two's apartment complex before overtime started at 1700. Perfect.

Morning Ryker immediately hit snooze. She cursed herself for drinking too much. Told herself she was lazy, and Felice was right. She couldn't tag FFP correctly. Why the hell did she think she could solve a murder? Murders.

After eighty-eight minutes of snoozing, Ryker knew she would hate herself if she didn't accomplish at least one of her pre-work goals. Four hours wasn't enough for a six-mile hike and snooping. It was enough for a walk around her neighborhood, with some added agility movements. Jumps, sprints, and a pull-up on the bars at the nearby park. The hoodie weighed heavily on her chest. The wind pierced through her cheeks and chapped her lips. A hike would have been terrible anyway.

The physical exertion calmed the negative thoughts in her head. Now she could focus on the day's primary task. Visiting the apartment complex felt premature, but they would be closed on Sunday. Monday was too far away. If she didn't harness her spite into action now, it would turn into apathy and a self-spiraling hate later.

Not knowing Eva's true identity prevented any connections between her and Desmund. Investigating these murders was similar to running an enzyme panel. Papain treated reagents enhance some reactions and destroy others. In her experience, the enzyme panel either answered all her questions or opened a can of worms. Rarely, the enzyme panel did nothing except waste some time and plasma.

This is either a good idea or plain stupid. I won't know until I do it.

"Hi, welcome to Egret Park. How may I help you?" The leasing agent sipped an orange liquid from a clear plastic cup. A twisty rubber key chain dangled from her wrist like a bracelet and clanged when she swirled her beverage.

"My name is Ryker. I had an appointment to view an apartment."

"Today?" She asked, taking another sip and tapping her nails against her keyboard. "Did you schedule online?"

"I scheduled it about an hour ago." Dampness collected under her armpits.

"Ohhhhh." The woman smiled big and stopped typing. "You see, my side of the schedule doesn't update until after midnight. It's a thing. We've told corporate. Luckily, I don't have anything on the books right now. Well, I did have brunch with my girls scheduled, but Brooke quit last night. Something about not feeling safe working alone on the weekends. So I took my brunch to go." She winked as she tapped on her cup. "I'm Lindsay. Would you like some brunch juice?"

"No thanks, I have to go to work today." As soon as she said it, Ryker realized brunch juice meant a screwdriver, and she sounded rude as hell. "I work at Drivers, I hand out blood, otherwise, I'd be all in."

"Oh, Drivers, yeah, we've got a few of y'all staying here. Are you another one of those weird peg-leg people? No offense."

"Am I a PiRat? No. Are there a lot here?"

"They have meetings in the poolhouse. They're crazy, but they clean up after themselves. Anyways, you won't find a better commute with a better pool. Avoid the poolhouse when their private party sign is up. I just need you to fill out this form, and I have to hang on to your *driver's* license while we look at your options. You see what I did there?" She pulled a complex map out of a file holder and placed it face up. "Available for us to view right now are a two bedroom and a one bedroom. The one bedroom does not have all the upgrades you'll see in the two bedroom, but we do have some upgraded one bedrooms that will be available in the next few weeks."

The two rooms were on opposite sides of the complex. "Sounds good," Ryker said as she forfeited her license.

"Great, follow me." Brunch juice in hand, Lindsay led Ryker to a golf cart and began the tour.

"Behind the leasing office is our pool. We don't officially close it at any time of the year, but it's not heated. Trust me, it gets very cold. We have two enclosures for dog parks and pet waste stations throughout. Yes, we do keep track of doo doo droppers."

The first apartment was a standard new apartment. Ryker felt bad for assuming they would be run down. The interior was clean and updated as promised. The ceilings weren't as tall as her current place, but she wasn't planning on moving, so she didn't point it out.

The second apartment, the non-updated one bedroom. That was the vision she had of a place so close to Drivers. Stained carpet, patchwork off white walls, cabinets with layers of paint thicker than the original pieces of wood. A odor not quite sweat, not quite smoke. Ryker wanted to ask the leasing agent about the death, but she wasn't sure how to bring it up.

"What made you want to check us out? Did you see us on your way into work or somewhere else?" She shook her drink as she brought the straw to her mouth. There was a smile not well hidden behind the melting ice of the near empty cup.

"Like you said, other people at Drivers stay here," Ryker paused, reading her reaction. "Then, I saw it on the news the other day."

"Ding, ding, ding. I'm not allowed to just tell people, but since you asked. Yes, that man was on his way here. His sister messaged me the video of her finding him. I'm sure you read her quote. I called the Drivers hotline with a tip, but no one followed up with me. Get this, earlier this week, this weird white lady showed up, asking a bunch of questions about how many people here work or are treated at Drivers. I told her I didn't know, and even if I did, I'm not giving that information away for free. Then she tried handing me some fake ID, couldn't even spell FBI right."

"She was an FDA inspector?"

"Those are real?"

"They are, but she wasn't. She's dead."

"Ghost?"

The cart swerved directly into a hedge of bushes. Lindsay stared at Ryker as if their current predicament was somehow her fault. Free of injuries, Ryker brushed away the leaves and twigs from her shoulder. Golf cart DUI accident was not on her Thanksgiving vampire murder mystery bingo card. "She was a fake FDA inspector. She died on Wednesday."

"Oh," she said over the safety beeps as she reversed onto the sidewalk. "Why'd you have to be all creepy about it?"

"Did she tell you her name?"

"We can check my calendar. She came on Tuesday. Alive."

On the drive back to the office, Elyssa walked along the sidewalk carrying bags of groceries. Ryker stared, unable to believe Elyssa had lived here the whole time and didn't say anything. A moment before they reached Elyssa's eyesight, Ryker turned her head and used the map to shield her face.

"Is that your ex?" Lindsay bumped into the curb as she parked the golf cart.

"Who?" Ryker was confused. "Desmund?"

"No, that girl we passed. I saw you duck and cover. Following them to their new apartment is a bold move. If you're interested, I know someone who likes her women with a bit of mayhem." She wafted her fingers at Ryker.

"I'm good. It was hard to tell in the light. If that was my ex, she lied about where she was moving." Ryker leaned into the assumption, no need to come up with a different excuse.

"Okay, stalker. Your secret is safe with me."

Inside the leasing office, Ryker waited as Lindsay pulled up her tours from Tuesday.

"Name, and a copy of her fake ass ID."

Eva Deluka, FDA.

Fucking can of worms.

Chapter 14

Current Day

*No **WONDER THERAPY SESSIONS** are only an hour. Talking at someone nonstop is exhausting. How do straight men do it?* Memories of her ex's voice penetrating her ears without consent cause her to groan.

"Am I bothering you?" Felice asks.

"It's not you, it's me. It's not some super passive-aggressive commentary about how annoyed I am you've got me locked in here and are forcing me to stay awake for over twenty-four hours."

"You wake up at 0300?"

"Eww. No. Why?"

"Do you need a break?"

"I need to pee."

"Were you going to tell me?"

"I was hoping you'd ask."

"I'll let you go first."

"You don't want to go at the same time? You think it'll diminish your authority if I know what your stream sounds like? I bet it's hard and fast." Ryker locks eyes with Felice.

She adjusts her blouse. Sign three.

"No worries. I'm sure your urine is just as intimidating as your face." Ryker laughs. "I'm so sorry, that was supposed to be a compliment." She places her hand on her chest as she catches her breath, "Can I have another coffee, too, please?"

"Still black?" Felice knocks on the door.

"Yes, ohh, can I get brown sugar this time? I like to do that as a treat."

Saturday: Five Days Ago

TWO MISSED CALLS FROM work during her tour at Egret Park. The first came with a voicemail. The second, nothing. Whatever Fatima wanted to talk to her about, it could wait until she was on the clock.

The smell of vanilla coffee met Ryker when she badged into the lab. Quinneth put something in the manual to-do rack. She didn't say anything, but the look on her face made Ryker want to investigate before Quinneth left.

"Why is this manual?" Ryker asked.

"The screen gave question marks."

"The instrument couldn't interpret the results. What did you do?"

"It gave question marks. I'm giving it to you."

"The machine could not interpret the results. Did you look at it? What do you think it is?"

"It's a question mark."

"Do you think it's positive and will need an antibody identification?"

"It's a question mark." Quinneth turned away, logged off the automated computer, and went to the storage room.

Ryker noticed the light on in Fatima's office, the door open, room empty. She stopped at the clean sink to wash her hands, giving Quinneth plenty of alone time in the storage room. People could call her mean all they wanted, but she was not going to let them accuse her of physical intimidation. She ensured they had ample personal space after interactions like these. Apparently, asking people to interpret the antibody screen they ran is insulting. As her therapist explained, when people are defensive, they assume you're on the attack.

The storage door closed the second time, Quinneth held her head down as she beelined for the exit. As if Ryker wanted to continue that riveting discussion. Focused on Quinneth's reaction, Ryker forgot about the phone calls. Fatima did not forget. She was waiting in the storage room. Not waiting, as in standing still. She was filing completed antibody review sheets.

"Good, you're here. Do you have a moment to talk to me in my office?" The standstill silence in the lab left no room for faking the need to sign into a computer first. Plus, two people currently in the lab were going to be there for at least another six hours, which meant turnover could also wait.

Ryker felt Wren and Rider's eyes as Fatima led her to the open office.

"I tried calling you, hopefully you got my message."

She got a message. She did not listen to it. She intended to do that on the clock. Silence was the best option.

"I already spoke to Yvette. I just need confirmation from you. Yesterday, the OR did not call about the units with the switched tags? They only returned them when the MTP was completed?"

"Yes. The last three digits were flipped. It's not a reportable dispensing error." One more thing Fatima is going to blame on her. It could have been June who switched the tags. Ryker was the one who initialed them as correct.

"Ryker, I've been in quality assurance for twenty years. I know what is and is not reportable. I don't have a problem with the MTP yesterday. My problem is you didn't tell me right away. OR is doing a system report, calling it a good catch on their end. My boss wakes me up freaking out because OR keeps saying mislabeled blood. It wasn't even blood, it was plasma. I told them we issued eighty-six products to this patient. The last forty-five products in twenty-five minutes. That's less than one minute per product. We were perfect on eighty-four of them. No one else can do those numbers. In the future, let me know if something like this happens so I'm not walking into a surprise on the weekend."

Ryker didn't know what to say. She'd never been yelled at and defended at the same time. "I understand. If something like that happens again, I will email you."

"Thank you, that's all I needed for that." Fatima pulled out a stack of incident reports. "You see how I was able to understand what happened without finding someone to blame."

The warm and fuzzies were fading.

"This is a serious reporting system. It's not a Yelp review." She laid her hand on the stack of papers.

"I am allowed to write any incident report in good faith."

"Is it good faith if you're the one at fault?" Fatima filed the reports and logged out of her computer. "That's all. Thank you for coming in tonight. We appreciate everything you do."

Ryker forced herself to leave the office. The dissociative rage felt like someone else controlled her body. Fatima still believed Ryker was the one making the mistakes. *Deep breaths, focus on easy work.*

Back at the manual workstation, Peg left a sample and noted it needed reflex units. Drivers policy mandates if there is no blood order on a patient with antibodies, then two units of red blood cells will be crossmatched after the antibody identification is completed. It mitigates delays. However, it's only necessary if the antibodies are clinically significant. Peg left reflexes on a passive Anti-D due to Rhogam, that antibody is eligible for electronic crossmatch. *Peg knows better. I must be missing something.*

Ryker was two guesses deep into the daily Wordle when Peg came back from lunch.

"Hey, did our policy change on reflexes?" Peg asked, not yet in her labcoat.

"No, I was going to ask you about that. It's just a Rhogam, right? We don't reflex for those."

"That's what I thought, but Quinneth told me we had to reflex all antibodies. She also said I was supposed to do gel crossmatch, but I thought if they were insignificant, we could do electronic?"

"You are correct. Do not listen to anything Quinneth says."

"Ok. I didn't want to argue with her in case something changed. It's hard to keep up with everything when we're only here on the weekends. She said something else I wanted to ask you about. Did we get new reagents?" Peg pointed to the analyzer.

"We got a new brand of the enzyme panel. Now it's the same as the 11-cell."

"Ok, uhm, but it's a separate panel, correct?"

"Yes?" Ryker had no idea where this was going.

"Quinneth said they were the same vials, and the instrument adds the enzyme."

Ryker did not intend to laugh as loud as she did. "That girl's entire brain is a question mark. I tried to tell them she can go through the motions, but she has no scientific grasp on what's happening."

"It sounded crazy, but again, we're not here every day."

"It's the same antigram. The non-treated 11-cell panel and the papain treated 11-cell panel. The lot numbers come in pairs. We document both on the same paper, so you can track the reaction changes. Like either destroyed or enhanced on cell number three. The factory pretreats the vials, like always. They are two different sets."

"All these new techs are confusing me." Peg put on her labcoat and logged into the automated station. After loading a couple of samples, she came back with a smirk on her face. "So what was Fatima doing here?"

Shit talking helped Ryker relax. The weekend crew were good people. Ryker told Peg about the mislabeled units, her chat with Fatima, and the other conversations she's had with Fatima this week.

"OR is patting themselves on the back because they're not the ones who messed up this time. There's no way Fatima thinks you're doing all that other stuff. I wonder what's going on with her?" Peg said exactly what Ryker needed in that moment. A solid session of information sharing is exactly why she signed up for overtime.

"Ryker, I'm sorry to interrupt, but a provider just ordered six cord blood workups. I found four of the samples, but I can't find the other two." Wren waved the orders in the air.

Ryker accompanied Wren up to the desk and walked her through finding the answer. "Oh, ok, yeah, it's because the samples haven't been collected yet."

"That's confusing. The order says *add-on*. You mean to tell me this baby is still inside the mom and they're ordering cord blood testing?"

"It was probably born a few minutes ago. They just haven't collected the sample in the computer. The doctors started doing this a few weeks ago. Liam thinks they updated the criteria for cord testing, but no one in Labor and Delivery will confirm.

"So what do we do? And why does it say add-on if there's nothing to add it to? Do I have to call somebody?"

"Call?" That's the laboratory C-word. "No. No. We haven't been calling anybody. We just wait for the sample to show up. Add-on is how they created the order in SAGA. They didn't want providers ordering cord blood workups on babies that didn't have a sample collected, so they made the test an add-on only."

"Some good that did if they can add it on to samples we don't have yet."

"Yup."

"Well, thank you. Quinneth had me and Peg thinking we didn't understand anything anymore. Then this happened. Glad to know I'm not going crazy."

"Oh yeah, I told Peg about the crossmatches."

"I heard y'all. I'm always hesitant to ask new people for help, because I'm supposed to know what I'm doing. Every week it feels like there's something new."

Wren, like Peg, had been with Driver's for a long time. When Ryker was fully trained and rotating into the weekends, she thought

Wren and Peg knew everything. She deferred to their judgment on most things. If you spend most of your career working without a supervisor, having to make decisions on your own, you've got to be a super tech, right? They were great. Not as all-knowing, all-powerful as Ryker assumed.

One night, while trying to troubleshoot one of the instruments, Peg asked Ryker if she knew how to clean the inside of the probe. A clotted sample left a bundle of red cells and fibrin, the size of a full pencil eraser, stuck to its tip. Tech support suggested she try cleaning it, *inside and out*, then call them back.

"I've only ever wiped the outside with an alcohol pad."

"Do you think we can find something small enough to poke the alcohol pad through the tip of the probe?" Peg asked.

"Oh yeah, I bet there's something in the toolbox." There was, and Ryker watched as Peg wrapped the pokey thing in an alcohol pad and shoved it up the tip of the probe. Clean.

They tried initializing the instrument, but the probe was not functioning. When Peg called tech support back, they asked if she removed the probe from the machine and rinsed it under deionized water for ten minutes. She confessed she did not. She did not know that's what they meant; she only cleaned it with alcohol.

It was on speaker phone. Tech support said, "Wiping the outside with alcohol is ok. As long as you did not attempt to insert or manipulate anything into the tip of the probe. That will damage the probe beyond repair. I'd have to send a technician out there to replace it."

Peg locked eyes with Ryker. Ryker shook her head. "We did not do that," Peg said. "We will run it underwater and call you back." Tech support must have been overdramatic. The operator's manual guided them through removing, cleaning, and replacing the probe. It was fine.

Breaking the rules together is the best way to bond with coworkers. Which rules they break, how they break them, and how they resolve them are important. There are standards. Don't enter quality controls into the LIS if you didn't perform them. Don't falsify patient testing. Never break the rules for someone who wouldn't be able to help you out of a pickle. Playing on the internet, handing someone a paper they forgot to initial, misleading tech support, those are team-building moments.

Ryker didn't wait for the two missing cord bloods to show up before starting her set. Who knew when or if those other samples would arrive? Of course, the forward type of one of the cord bloods displayed mixed field. She repeated the testing, washing the blood six times with saline. Still mixed field.

"Hi, this is Ryker in transfusion. Are you the nurse for Baby Boy Royster...We're getting inconclusive results on the cord blood testing...Most likely, the sample is contaminated with blood from the mother...I will have to cancel all three tests, the type, the confirm type, and the DAT...If the provider still wants the testing, they will need to order a heel stick workup and have that sample collected. Thanks."

Ryker plowed through the New York Times games within her first hour. She tried searching the internet for other Eva Delukas. She even signed up on one of those sketchy sites that do background checks. No sign of anyone who looked like their Eva.

"Ryker," Wren held a blood order. "Dr. Kudela requested an irradiation requirement for this patient, but they already had a unit crossmatched. Do we need to uncrossmatch it to irradiate it?"

"We can irradiate the unit, then update it. I can show you." Ryker took the unit out of the fridge, placed a rad sure sticker on it, and fired up the irradiator. "Did he give a reason for the requirement?"

"I didn't ask." Wren said, "I got tired of fighting these residents years ago. They wanna add irradiated, I give them irradiated."

Last night was too busy to investigate why the hell Dr. Kudela was handing out irradiation requirements like he was Oprah. This was Ryker's chance to see what the hell his obsession was about. The patient was in the ICU, diagnosis of sepsis following a heart attack. Neither is an indication for irradiation. Was there something wrong with their white blood count? More wrong than sepsis.

Their total white count was high, increased neutrophils, decreased lymphocytes. Maybe there were some blasts or precursor cells noted on the differential? Then she saw it, like a blue-green beacon in the night. Death crystals. Why would crystals be treated with irradiated blood? Something wasn't adding up.

"Did he add it to any more today?" Ryker asked, sifting through the pending orders.

"Not with me, but there are a few I noticed with irradiation requirements." Wren sat at her station and opened a news tab. She was not interested in whatever trouble Ryker was digging up.

"He approved one for me earlier," Rhyder said. "He was extra snippy. Then he realized I said Rhyder, and he de-escalated." Over the phone, people mistook Ryker's name for Rhyder. When Drivers hired someone named Rhyder, it turned out she had the same, but opposite problem. Rhyder's twelve-hour shift started at 1100. On the weekends, when they both worked, the amount of "was I just talking to you" confusion skyrocketed. It wasn't confusing for Ryker or Rhyder; they enjoyed the sprinkling of chaos. "Are you pestering the baby residents with your insufferable questions and being right all the time, again?"

She was the newest to the weekend crew, but she fit in perfectly. Fresh out of college, her first job as a med tech, Rhyder was crushing it. Not only did she ask questions, she remembered the answers. She knew policies existed, and she could find information in them.

"Does it help my case if he was making weird faces at me?" Ryker asked. *Who else but a vampire would think it's normal to protrude their tongue out of their face like it's a meerkat on guard duty? Why is he adding irradiation requirements to so many patients?*

Patient one: heart attack and sepsis, no antibodies, crystals this morning.

Patient two: alcoholic ketoacidosis and fatty liver disease, no antibodies, no crystals.

Hmmmm.

Under normal circumstances, Ryker would call Dr. Sanders and ask him if he knew his resident was going cowboy. It was still an option, but not one Ryker wanted to play just yet. Something wasn't adding up.

Fatima, in her generosity, brought in donuts on her trip to yell at Ryker. A handwritten note on the outer lid read, "Thanks for all that you do." Nothing gets the gears turning better than sugar and fried dough.

Three options lined the box. Plain glaze, chocolate iced, and blueberry cake. Plain glaze may be boring to some, but for Ryker, it's the litmus test for a donut shop. The glaze flaked off the dough and melted in her mouth. The bread was sweet and fluffy. Most importantly, the glaze covered the top and bottom of the donut. No dry bite for the entirety. This deserved a celebratory second donut. And a managerial coffee.

While Fatima made claims of Ryker not being accountable, she forgot to close Liam's office when she left. The supervisors pitched in and bought an espresso machine, kept under lock and key, or the watchful gaze of their director. They never outright stated techs weren't allowed to use it, but they also never invited them for a cup.

As the coffee brewed, Ryker took a moment to take in the essence of Liam. She'd been in his office plenty of times, but never with this much freedom. Most of the drawers were boring. Paperclips, pens, sticky notes, an earring found in the bathroom. She wasn't snooping for anything in particular. It's not like he'd leave a termination notice for Quinneth on his desk for Monday.

Sitting in his chair, office lights off, the view of the lab through the opened blinds gave Ryker goosebumps. Like she was watching a horror movie, waiting for the jump scare. *Does a vampire bite hurt?* Desmund's wounds sounded agonizing. *What if the vampire isn't someone who works here? What if it's someone living in the walls or ceiling?*

"Errrgggg."

She kicked the seat back, nearly falling out.

A soothing chime and flashing lights announced the birth of a fresh cup of espresso.

"God dammit, brain."

The chair struggled to return to its original position. Something wrapped itself around the wheels. Ryker tugged, firm but not forceful. It didn't budge. She tapped the light switch and reexamined the problem. It was a strap. Connected to a bag, a nice leather satchel. After unwinding the bag from the wheel, she placed it back in the corner.

The coffee was amazing. A dark, bitter brew with a hint of earth notes. She helped herself to another donut. The blueberry cake dipped in the coffee tasted like a dream. It was almost good enough to forgive Fatima's false accusations. Almost.

She considered another donut. *Why not try all the flavors?* The pain in her stomach answered for her. "Time to clean up the evidence," she said. The thought drew her eye to the leather bag.

He wouldn't. Would he?

She had to make sure. Inside the bag was a notebook, a mini plastic banana, chopsticks, and a bottle of hand sanitizer.

Chapter 15

"EVA DELUKA?" HE ASKED.

"Isn't it perfect?" She held the fake FDA badge up to her face and smiled.

Her younger brother had always been more cautious, even before their mom died. Too scared to break the rules. Heartbroken when he disappointed anyone. "You used your real name. Aren't fake identities supposed to be, I don't know, fake?"

"That's the genius of it. If you mess up and call me Eva, no one will notice. Plus, the last name is different." She put her arm around his shoulders, forcing him to continue judging the badge.

"I don't like it," he sighed.

"It's the perfect cover for me to get the final piece of evidence we need to take this vamp out." Eva threw a right hook.

"I asked you not to use that word. They aren't cool, mysterious creatures of the night. They're murderers. I'm so close. I don't think we should risk exposing ourselves."

"Vamp is a no, but you get to talk about us like we're a couple of trench coat flashers?" Eva laughed.

"Why aren't you bringing your cell phone? What if this goes wrong, and you need backup?"

"I'm committing fraud. You don't bring your phone to crimes."

"Fine. I still think this is a bad idea." Her brother left his kitchen and retreated to his bedroom.

Eva and her brother spend every Thanksgiving together. Not because either one of them makes a great turkey. To be fair, it's hard to season food with a garlic allergy. They never said it outright, but they know why they make this time for each other. It's the anniversary of their mom's death.

He spent the last six months tracking a vampire feeding from patients at Drivers. All they needed now was to uncover the vampire's identity.

EVA COULDN'T BELIEVE HOW easy it was to get into Drivers. She had access to the entire blood bank and the other labs. She'd been around an FDA inspection once or twice. Completed inspection reports were available online. Eva created a blank document to mirror real reports, and filled it in as she went.

The plan was to lay low, not call out anything too harsh. Then she met Quinneth. Keeping a struggling employee is fine, as long as you give them ample support. Eva pressed Quinneth enough for her manager to see that signing people off as competent and hoping they get better over time is not a viable improvement strategy. No reason she couldn't be a helpful criminal.

After Quinneth's train wreck of an irradiation process, she sat with Fatima in the conference room next door to the blood bank, pretending to scour logs and documentation for accuracy.

"Hello, hope you don't mind an interruption for a few minutes? My name is Dr. Sanders, I'm the Blood Bank Medical Director. This is my resident, Dr. Kudela. Feel free to contact me if there is anything you need during your visit."

Eva put the hard copy policy folder on the table. She squirted a bit of hand sanitizer on her hands and offered it to Dr. Sanders. "Thank you. Eva Deluka."

He took her hand into his with a firm grasp. "How long will we be hosting the FDA, Ms. Deluka?" The warmth from his palm transferred to hers.

"I'll definitely be back tomorrow. I might be here a third day."

"Twenty-four hours," Fatima said.

"I'm not sure I follow," Eva said.

"The FDA can only perform surprise inspections for a twenty-four-hour period. They implemented the rule at the beginning of this year. Labs need time to provide adequate staffing if inspections will be longer." Fatima handed her a new binder. "That is, unless the lab is found deficient."

"I have made four observations, so far."

"Not all have been severe. We corrected one observation on site." If it weren't blowing her cover, Eva would be impressed. She'd prepped for weeks to be a fake FDA inspector. It wasn't enough to match this quality assurance expert.

Dr. Kudela's tongue flashed out of the corner of his mouth.

Eva laughed. A big, loud, harsh laugh. "Apologies, that's a little joke I like to play when I do surprise inspections. It usually lands."

That got a big laugh from Dr. Sanders. Dr. Kudela's tongue retreated.

Towards the end of her day at Drivers, Eva admitted her brother had a point. She was no closer to discovering the vampire's identity. *It's Thanksgiving. Committing fraud is exciting at first, but in the long run, it's nothing compared to spending quality time with her brother. After all, that's what the holiday is all about.*

The bathroom door groaned open. Someone entered the stall next to hers. Probably that one tech, Ryker. *She trailed me down the hall.* Silence from her new neighbor. She rolled her eyes. *Ryker can't even pee without being weird. What if she doesn't have to pee? I should hurry.*

As she washed her hands, a glance in the mirror confirmed she was alone. Chills traveled up her spine and across her arms. *I know someone came in.* The paper towel dispenser hollered. Eva nearly lost her footing.

"One day undercover and you're already having jump scares in the bathroom," she said, scowling at her salmon pink lip stain and brown eye shadow.

The pre-dispensed towel lay in a puddle of water on the counter. Eva tore that one off and let it fall through the trash hole. She wafted her hand in front of the red motion sensor light, but nothing happened. Frustrated, she cursed the dispenser and turned for the door.

A person stood two sinks away. No reflection in the mirror.

"What are you doing here?" Her eyes shifted from the mirror to the person.

"I was going to ask you the same thing."

Before she could move, her mouth was covered and her neck bent.

Deep inhale through their nose. "Banana is a unique scent, but not potent enough to stop me. Now, be a good girl," they whispered in her ear.

She wondered why victims never appeared to fight back. No skin fragments under the nails, no offensive wounds. The bite not only drain her blood, it drained her will to live. As she hung powerless in this grasp, she thought about the promise she made to their mom to keep her brother safe. She had one last thing up her sleeve. Literally. A silver cuff link forged to look like a wooden stake.

It burned into her attacker's neck, causing them to drop her. She reached into her jacket, her heart sank.

"Looking for these?" They broke the chopsticks with one hand. "You vampire hunters are all the same. You think you can waltz into my world and take me out. There's a reason you don't have a union. Not enough survivors."

Eva threw one final punch. Her hand was caught and gently maneuvered out of the way, not breaking any bones. She relaxed into defeat. Everything went black.

Chapter 16

Current Day

"**How did you know** it was Eva's?" Felice asks.

"One of the pages in the notebook had notes from her inspection. Lots of opinions about Quinneth." Ryker says.

"Why do you think Liam the bag after the police asked for it?"

Ryker pawed at the bag of baby carrots like a cat playing with a mouse. But the mouse is already dead, and the cat is sad and bored and hitting it, hoping to find that spark of joy in the chase once more.

"I asked for a snack, not an intervention. Where did you find these? Even Drivers isn't cruel enough to put carrots in a vending machine."

The late night, the talking, the bad coffee, shoving chopsticks in her friend's chest, finding new ways to annoy Felice, all of it intertwined in Ryker's stomach. Cookies, chips, coffee cake. She needed comfort food, sugar, salt, not beta-carotene for fuck's sake.

"You want a better snack, I want to know your thoughts on Liam keeping Eva's property." Felice took a bite of carrot. Her smirk expanded with each crunch.

"Fiiiiiinnnnne." She squeezes the back of her neck. "Liam is infatuated with quality leather goods. Sunny complimented him on his work bag once. He spent ten minutes telling us how he contacted the company to ask if they could make him a custom laptop case. They did. The next day, he brought in their brochure and discussed every item. My guess is he wanted it."

"Why not take it home?"

"Plausible deniability? If the police find it in his home, at worst, he's a prime murder suspect. At best, he's charged with tampering with evidence. Left in his office, he could easily say he didn't know it was there. I rolled over it in five minutes. Liam knew he had it. Most likely, he was hoping the investigation would be resolved without it, and then he'd take it home."

"You didn't think Liam could be the vampire?"

"False. I already told you I suspected everyone. If you're wondering about the moral integrity of someone who keeps evidence from police for personal use, the bag didn't kill her. Nothing in there would have helped them discover her identity. If anything, knowing he snubs authority went into the pro column."

Sunday: Four Days Ago

"ANDY, HOW BUSY ARE you? I need a favor."

Ryker got as much information as she could from the blood bank LIS. Eva had a list of patient names in her notebook. They all had different blood types, even an AB pos. Most didn't have antibodies, one patient had an anti-E. The dates next to each name went back six months. If there was a common thread, Ryker couldn't find it. At least, not based on blood bank alone.

Ryker took a chance and ventured to the STAT lab on Saturday night, no Andy. Their schedule listed him working on Sunday. As luck would have it, the blood bank still needed coverage for Sunday night. Another six-hour shift to find a killer vampire? Easy yes.

"Hey, Sis. This isn't your regular weekend rotation." Andy raised his head from the microscope.

"Overtime." She nodded, feeling guilty for not knowing Andy's weekends. "Not to be too mysterious, but if I gave you a list of names, do you think you could give me their results off the machines?"

"Capable, yes. Willing, depends. How long is the list, and how fast do you need them?" Andy wheeled his chair closer to Ryker.

She handed him a copy of the page from Eva's book. "I only have a fifteen-minute break, so ten minutes?"

"Are you working with Dr. Kudela?" Andy walked towards a stack of files.

"What do you mean?"

"I made him copies of all the same records. He's writing a paper about the blue-green crystal-like neutrophilic inclusions."

"Death Crystals? Why? When did he ask for these?" Ryker's brain was firing on all fronts. She had a dozen more questions, but forced herself to let Andy answer before she jumped the gun any further.

"Yes. Research. It started a month ago."

"All those patients had crystals in their blood?"

"Yeah, well, that last name listed, Nwadike, he had crystals on his initial admission to the ER. Then, after his blood exchange, they disappeared."

"What about when he came back, as a trauma patient?"

"After the animal attack? I heard he was too, mutilated, to draw blood."

"So they're all dead? All these crystal patients?"

"We got a new one this morning, I emailed Dr. Kudela the results when my shift started."

"We added an irradiation requirement to them this afternoon. Andy, do you know what this means?" Ryker skimmed the stacks of papers.

"I have no idea what's happening in your head right now." Andy took the files and returned them to their designated spot.

"Kudela is a vampire," Ryker's voice carried over the lab.

Andy scrunched his face.

"Facts," Ryker said equally as loud before she remembered other people could hear and perceive her. "Fact, he's allergic to garlic.

Fact, he does a weird thing with his tongue. The crystals are how he chooses his victims. Kudela knows they have a low twenty-four-hour survival rate. It's the perfect crime. I bet he's been feeding off our patients since his residency started. That's why he killed Eva."

"I have a question. Are you ok?"

"Oh, right, you don't know any of this. Why don't you work in blood bank so I don't have to explain as much? Anywho, Eva, our fake FDA inspector. She came here after we reported an improperly labeled irradiated unit. Then she died. I saw the bite marks on her neck. One hundred percent vampire. Then Dr. Kudela started adding irradiation requirements to all these people who don't need it. Yesterday I found Eva's bag. She had this list of names, and guess what else, chopsticks. Not bamboo. Wooden chopsticks. She's a vampire hunter who came here to stop Kudela from playing god and taking the lives of patients. He must have uncovered her true identity and killed her first."

"What I'm hearing is you found evidence in a murder investigation and..."

"Identified the killer." Ryker finished his sentence.

"And you tampered with it." Andy was dead serious.

"I didn't tamper with anything, I just looked through it. It was in Liam's office, if anyone's going to get in trouble..."

"Ryker, stop," Andy's voice soft but stern. "I don't want to be involved with this. Two people are dead, you can't just say the word vampire and expect me to jump on board. I know you want to work for the SSB. Sis, this is not how you get there. Actions have consequences."

"I'm not making this up."

"Last month, you tried to convince me our new COO was a demon because his official Drivers portrait was blurry."

She wanted to be upset. Release the Kraken. This was Andy. Not some dingbat first shift tech. Deep breath. "You're right about the evidence thing. I'll call the hotline and report it tomorrow. Something is happening here. I'm going to get to the bottom of it. With or without your help." Ryker hovered. She called, but Andy wasn't bluffing.

"Is this about last year?" he asked.

"You sound like Yvette."

"So I'm not the only one who noticed? Have you taken PTO since the outbreak? Did you find a new therapist yet?"

"That's out of line."

"It's not. I'm worried about you. Work isn't a coping strategy. The timing has to have an impact."

Last year, last Thanksgiving, that was the day Ryker decided to leave her husband. Years of turbulent fighting, lying, and manipulation came together in front of both their families. He made a comment during dinner, suggesting they might have kids one day, causing their mothers to swoon. She told him a week before she didn't want children. A realization she had during therapy. He said he supported her choice and would be more than happy to live child-free with her for the rest of his life.

"Why would you say that?" She called him out in front of everyone. "We talked about this. I don't want to have kids. You agreed with me."

"Accidents can happen, love. Like I've always said, if it does, it would be a blessing."

"I'm on the pill. I take it diligently. There will be no accident. You know this."

"Come on, don't be like that, we're at the dinner table."

"Don't be like what? You're the one lying to our parents. I'm trying to understand why you would say that."

"How dare you accuse me of lying in front of family. I hold my honor sacred, you know that. That's really hurtful."

"You just asked my mom if she wanted *cran cran* to be her grand-mother name."

"Ryker, sweets, it's ok. Let's just have a nice dinner," her mom said.

"Yeah, he didn't promise grandchildren," her sister chimed in, "He was making a joke."

"Would you like some pie, dear?" his mom asked.

"No, thank you, I'm going to go for a walk." Ryker made it outside and down the front steps.

"Hey," her husband called. "How dare you talk to me like that in front of everyone?"

"I can't do this," she said. "I'm very upset. I need a few minutes to myself."

"We're having this conversation now," he said. "I'm tired of you always running away when I need to talk to you."

"My needs are important too. I need time. I need to go on a walk. Alone." She turned.

"You'll listen when I'm talking to you," he said.

She felt a tug on her arm. Rage channeled through her fist. As he pulled her towards him, she swung. It landed on his left cheek. He pushed her. She fell hard against the concrete.

"What's wrong with you?" he asked, opening the door.

An hour later, when she got back from her walk, they stared at her like she had grown a second head. No one saw him grab her. No one heard him behind the front door. They never saw the other fights. They never saw him follow her around the house, braking down the doors she hid behind, demanding her to listen. They weren't there when she woke up the mornings after. They didn't see him sitting on the floor next to her side of the bed drinking coffee so he knew the moment her eyes opened. They didn't see the scrape on her wrist from hitting the concrete. Everyone saw the bruise on his face. Everyone heard her screaming, "Go cry to your fucking mother," as he entered the house. They made up their minds about what happened without hearing her side.

"This isn't about that, Andy," Ryker said. Allowing her breath to keep time with the mechanical symphony. "I'll let you get back to work."

What the hell is going on with him and Yvette? Are they forgetting about the episode of The Walking Dead we survived? There's an entire fucking government agency called the Specialists in Supernatural Beings, and they're shunning me for mentioning vampires. God dammit. Back to working with the one person I can sort of count on, me.

Different colors of pies hung on the walls of the STAT lab. Each pie covered with a sheet protector to comply with OSHA regulations. Ryker couldn't remember the last time she came in here over Thanksgiving. Was this on par with their normal attempts at decorating? A rotund orange pumpkin sat atop one of the chemistry analyzers. Its tail feathers and pilgrim hat were much more ornate than the ones scattered throughout Drivers. Gold weaved throughout the jewel-toned plumage.

"Pretty." Ryker pointed to the makeshift turkey.

"Yarr." The chemistry tech winked.

His response gave her pause. Another look at the feathers. The gold trim around the eye of each tail feather formed the symbol for Pi.

"You can't be serious?" Ryker fumed at the chemistry tech. "If you saw the carnage left in here that night, you wouldn't be so happy to support that piece of shit."

"Mind your business, landlubber." He turned his back on her.

"Landlubber. Fucking landlubber." All the patience she gathered with Andy was thrown overboard. "I spent four years in the Navy. I earned two sea service ribbons, my ESWS, and crossed the equator as both a pollywog and a shellback. You suck some Pi pricks taint and think you can call yourself a pirate? I have a stuffed kola bear that's more salty than all you nut guzzlers combined."

Andy moved between Ryker and the chemistry tech. "This isn't the place. I think your fifteen is over."

"I've got a kola bear you can stuff." The chemistry tech shouted as the lab door shut behind her.

Not only was he an asshole, he was also an idiot. That comeback made no sense. She wanted to knock that stupid pumpkin off the analyzer. She wanted to rip those ugly pies off the walls. No. No. What she needed to do was drive a stake through someone's heart. She knew exactly who, and she had the chopsticks in her pocket to do it.

Chapter 17

Current Day

"Can you blame them for thinking you had displaced feelings? No one wanted Eva around, she was difficult to work with, and when she died no one cared. What's more possible, vampires or Ryker seeing herself as the victim?"

"I mean, fuck you. Also, those things aren't mutually exclusive. They might have been right about me projecting a little. But I was right about the vampire."

"That's your takeaway. You were right?"

"One hundred percent. Who needs friends or families or husbands when you believe in yourself?"

Sunday: Four Days Ago

"DID YOU GO SEE Andy?" Peg raised her eyebrows. She declared Andy had a crush on Ryker the first time Ryker mentioned his name. Ryker tried explaining, but Peg wasn't hearing it.

Ignoring the bait that would lead to letting go of this anger, Ryker logged into SAGA and paged the on-call resident.

The residents didn't hang out in the blood bank. Their office was somewhere on the third floor of the general lab building. Plus, it was a weekend. There was no guarantee Vampire Kudela was even on campus.

The phone rang, she snagged it.

"Transfusion, this is Ryker..." She thought it was the resident calling back. It was a nurse. She had to put on her nice voice. "...That patient has an active warm auto antibody, any blood we give them will be labeled as incompatible...No matter who it comes from...We appreciate the offer, let's hope that doesn't become necessary."

"Let's hope what doesn't become necessary?" Rhyder peeked her head over the automated workstation.

"Our Labor and Delivery lady with the warm auto? Her husband is concerned that the blood tag says incompatible. He claimed his sister-in-law has the same blood type as his wife. He offered her blood for our use."

"Ok wow," Rhyder waved her hand. "Is the sister here to agree, or is the husband, like, offering to get us that blood?"

"I could not tell, but I don't want him to go rogue. I left it at let's hope that doesn't become necessary."

A tube fell into the station, Peg emptied its contents onto the end table. "What do you do when you get these?" She held a small bag with a pill inside. "Do you call the floor or send it back?"

"Neither," Ryker smiled at the opportunity to let out some petty energy. "I send it to pharmacy. I like to imagine the pharmacy tech getting the pills back and thinking something was discontinued or the patient didn't want it. Then the nurse calls irate because they're late giving their patient meds. Then the pharmacy asks them why they sent it back if they needed to give it. Then they investigate, and the nurses get written up for carelessness."

"Wow, you think all of that happens?" Peg searched the tube station's directory for the pharmacy and hit send.

"A girl can dream." Ryker yawned, releasing the rest of the anger she carried away from the STAT lab. "What do you know about Dr. Kudela?"

"He's one of our residents, right?" Peg shrugged, "Why? What do you know about Dr. Kudela?"

"Not enough. Do you still have access to online newspapers? I have a feeling he's not who he says he is." Ryker needed to give Peg some details. Not all of them. After Felice's and Andy's response, she'd keep the vampire in the coffin this time.

"You think he's involved with the FDA woman?" Peg hurried to her workstation. "Yes, I have access. Am I searching him or her first?"

"Are we internet stalking?" Rhyder chimed in, "I call TikTok and Insta."

"He's my age, so you might want to check Facebook," Ryker added.

"Heard." Rhyder's thumbs were already in sport mode.

Ryker had five days left on her 7-day free trial, she might as well make the most of it.

In a little over twenty minutes, Ryker found nothing helpful. Without his birthplace and birthday, the records website was useless. Peg found one obituary with the last name Kudela. A woman survived by her two children and husband. It's possible the vampire married a human woman. Ryker couldn't fathom the biology of vampires having swimmers or their viability in a human womb. Also, "My stepdad is a vampire," sounded too much like a teen horror movie.

"Biiiiiish," Rhyder let out a wail like a timer. "This is totally him, right?" She held up her phone.

A profile photo of a young guy in a graduation cap and gown. "It's hard to tell," Ryker squinted.

"There's only one way to find out." Peg wiggled with enthusiasm.

Deep breath. Ryker used social media, but not well. Less than a hundred followers on Instagram, slightly more on Facebook. She has never friend-requested a stranger. She would spend days debating whether to send requests to people she knew. *Maybe they don't remember me? Maybe they do and are avoiding me? I don't want to seem desperate.*

Request sent.

Phone rings.

Ryker, Rhyder, and Peg scream.

"Transfusion, this is Wren...let me put you on hold for a minute. ..Did anyone page the resident?"

"Ryker did," Rhyder giggled.

"Transfusion, this is Ryker," she said with as much pep as she could muster.

"This is the transfusion medicine services resident. I'm returning a page." His voice acting on par with Ryker's.

With an audience of ears perked and ready for dropping eaves, Ryker wished she had planned a script before paging. "I'm sure you heard Eva, our FDA inspector, did not work for the FDA."

"I did."

"I know what she was doing here, and I think you know it, too."

Silence on the line.

Ryker continued. "Eva was looking for someone. I think they got to her first."

"Did you just send me a friend request?" Kudela's calm and chipper tone gave way to almost panic. "Are you toying with me? After what you did?"

"After what I did?" Ryker whisper-yelled. "I know it was you. I'm going to prove it. You're done here."

"If it weren't for you, she'd still be alive," bitterness filled his words. "You'd better watch your back, you're in way over your head."

"What about all the patients, all the other people? Are you going to blame me for not stopping you from killing them, too? I've got more than garlic up my sleeve for you, bloodsucker."

A long pause. "Do you have anything to triage?" Kudela asked.

"No." Ryker shifted through the new pages on the printer. "Oh, wait, I do. ICU ordered one unit of FFP." Ryker read the name and MRN.

"I'll get back to you with this triage as soon as possible." That's what that lying, homicidal, weird-tongued Dr. Vampire Kudela said over an hour ago. It was 2047, and the floor called twice already asking for the plasma. *Maybe he ran off? Maybe I scared him enough that he's running to another hospital in another part of the country? Let him have Florida blood. I'm sure they've got worse.*

As the night carried on, Ryker's hope of abandonment turned into fear for the people in the ICU. What if she showed her cards too soon? What if instead of hiding, Kudela was ruthlessly draining the life out of Drivers' most vulnerable patients?

She paged again. One, to gauge his mental state. Two, the nurse wanted that FFP. Ten minutes later, no response.

Time to do her favorite thing in this situation, page his boss. Dr. Sanders called before the minute changed.

"Hi, Dr. Sanders, this is Ryker. We've been waiting over an hour for an FFP triage, the floor keeps calling, Dr. Kudela hasn't returned any follow-up pages...Thanks."

He called back shortly, "Dr. Kudela is not responding to my texts or calls. If he's not dead, he'll wish he was soon. I'm at our annual Director's Dinner. I missed the keynote speech. In the meantime, that FFP is approved."

2105, she had the perfect solution to two problems. By bringing the FFP upstairs for an audit, Ryker could ensure Dr. Kudela wasn't stealing blood from the patient he marked with the irradiation requirement. Also, issuing the unit in a cooler meant she didn't have to call to see if the nurse was still ready to transfuse.

Bright lights, nurses passing in the hall, nothing out of the ordinary. Each patient's door had a different fall flavor latte cup made from poster board. Matching foliage draped from the cups down the door. The lack of pies brought comfort. At least some people in this place had their heads on straight.

The transfusion started without a hitch. The nurse performed every item on the checklist like she'd done it that way a hundred times. As Ryker left, she peered at the rooms of the other patients for clues, or vampires.

"Did you need anything else? That patient doesn't have a transfusion order for tonight." It was the same nurse from the audit.

"Sorry, I think I got turned around." Ryker pretended to check the room number for guidance.

"I'm really tired of you blood bankers lingering in my hallways. It doesn't matter what study you are doing. My patients have rights."

She folded her arms across her chest, waiting for Ryker to find her exit.

The first thing she checked when she returned to the lab was the running audit list. November documented one other trip to the ICU. Ryker assumed his vampire powers allowed Dr. Kudela to pass through the rooms unnoticed. It made sense for him to have an excuse ready in case he got caught. The research paper gave him access to patient charts. It also gave him physical access to patient rooms.

"I think I know why Dr. Kudela hasn't called us back." Wren stood at the service window in the hallway. Sans labcoat, work bag and car keys in hand.

"Didn't you leave?" Ryker blurted out. She meant to ask, "Is everything ok? Why did you come back in the lab after you clocked out?" but sometimes her brain speaks shorthand.

"Yeah, I was going to clock out when I saw someone passed out in the breakroom. He's in dress clothes. I heard Peg saying she couldn't get a hold of anybody. Not that I want to spread any rumors, but he might be drunk."

Rhyder drew the short straw for who had to stay in the lab. At a level one trauma center, the one time everyone leaves the lab for three minutes, that's when multiple casualties pull into the Emergency Room. Ryker had experience with this sort of thing. Wren was clocked out. Peg was lead, she was going to be the one to report his ass.

"There, see, he still hasn't moved," Wren said. A man sat slumped over at one of the tables with a sheath of slides.

"Don't go in." Ryker mom-armed Wren from stepping inside, "That's exactly how Javier acted."

The door slammed closed. They waited for the man to move. Nothing.

"You think it's another outbreak?" Peg asked.

"Either way, I'm going home once we find out." Wren parked her rolling bag outside the door.

"I'll go in." Ryker grabbed the door handle.

"I'll go with you." Peg put her hand on Ryker's shoulder.

"We're all going in." Wren fit her keys so that they were sticking out between the fingers of her clenched fist.

Everyone inside, the man still didn't move. Ryker tried knocking on the door. Nothing. She picked up a chair and let it fall to the ground. Nothing.

"Dr. Kudela," Wren shouted. Nothing.

There was a broom in the corner by the door. Plastic, short, not great in fight, barely had a longer reach than Peg, but it would have to work. Ryker inched towards the man, his cheeks in direct contact with his slides. Peg and Wren stood side by side, a step behind Ryker.

When they got within broom's length, Ryker pressed his shoulder with the broom. Nothing. She pressed harder. Nothing.

"Let me try," Peg suggested.

She was lead, so Ryker handed her the broom. She swung a chair in between Peg and the man as a physical barrier. Peg jabbed the broom, she missed his shoulder. The momentum brought her forward. She landed on the empty chair, and it skidded into the man's legs. He moved forward, his face landing in the nape of Peg's neck.

Peg screamed. Ryker shoved the man off her.

"I told y'all. Dead drunk." Wren said as she tapped his foot with hers.

"Not drunk. Just dead." Skin pale, dried blood stained the collar of his shirt. Two puncture marks on his neck. Unless this was vampire-on-vampire crime. Ryker had gotten the whole thing wrong. Fuck.

"Not to be insensitive." Peg grimaced as she straightened her scrubs. "But should I call the emergency line, or the non-emergency line? He's already dead. I don't want to inconvenience anyone."

"911, hundred percent," Ryker said, staring at the body. Next to a pile of slides, a word written in blood. Ryker gulped.

"I'm going home." Wren shook her hair out of her face, put her key bracelet around her wrist.

"The cops will want to talk to you, they don't like it when we assault the actual dead."

"Tell them I'm turning my phone off tonight, but I'll call them back in the morning if they leave a voicemail." She filled up her tumbler with ice, then walked out.

"Should one of us wait with the body? Is that a thing?" Peg shrugged.

"You can go back to the lab, I'll stay, make sure he's still dead when the police get here."

She wanted to be standing casually when the police came, but her body couldn't remember a natural posture. Not only did she have the victim's purse from one murder at home, she erased evidence from another. She couldn't leave, "Sis," waiting for the cops to see. What if they accused Andy? Andy, who lets spiders live freely in his house. Andy, who decided to remain a conscientious objector during The Last of Us. He did not kill Dr. Kudela. Neither did Ryker. Why did he write Andy's nickname for her as his dying clue?

"He's in here." Rhyder's voice traveled down the hall.

Ryker stood at Navy rest, hands behind her back, legs apart, knees bent. That's the important part, so you don't faint. Knees bent and not having a three-hour-long retirement ceremony, outside, in the middle of the summer, in Texas.

"O M G," Rhyder mouthed after she peeked at the scene.

"We're going to close this place off for a bit," one of the officers said. "Do all of you work in," he eyed their badges, "Transfusion?"

"Yes." They said in unison. Rhyder unable to hide her excitement. Ryker in her flat business tone.

"Someone will be in to talk to you ladies soon." He joined the others in the breakroom.

"I've never seen a dead body before, not like, in the wild. Wait. Do I need to delete my search history? Is it a crime to internet stalk someone the same day they die?"

"Unless they ask directly, we won't mention it. Pretty sure Peg will be on board with leaving out any self-incriminating statements."

Ryker's phone buzzed. The text preview showed Wren asking Ryker to verify that she updated QC correctly. Underneath was a Facebook notification, "Friend request accepted."

Chapter 18

WEEK THREE, SUNNY REPORTED for her last introductory training department: Quality Assurance.

Gladson jumped out of his seat when she entered the lab. "Congrats! They asked me to escort you to the final workspace. I know what you're thinking. Yes, they asked me. I did not volunteer. I'm totally still mad you didn't try my banana bread."

It wasn't fair. Sunny wanted to feel her excitement, to giggle, and high-five, like she did with Nevasha. She knew if she displayed any of that around Gladson, he'd weaponize it to do something creepy. "Let's get going."

"You worked in a blood bank before, right?"

"Yeah." She didn't want to be alone with him. The halls were always empty during her escorts, she was used to that. If she screamed, would anyone hear?

"Yes, I remembered." He air-tooted his own horn. "And it was Drivers?"

"Yup." She hoped this would complete their chit chat, but Gladson persisted.

"Wow. Don't want to dish on your old employer. I can respect that." It was clear now, he was reading from a script and waiting for her to give the prescribed response. She did her best to be cordial yet noncompliant.

"I mean, you guys all know about the outbreak. That's why I'm here."

"Well, yeah, silly. It's not gossip if I already know. Come on, you had to have an annoying coworker or two."

"Did we go in a circle? We just passed the lab." The plaque on the door was familiar.

Gladson ignored her concern, "You'd think so, but no. Isn't it frustrating how all the hallways and doors look alike? Almost like they're designed to get people lost."

"Are you stalling?" Sunny put a few steps of distance between herself and Gladson.

"I give up." He held his hands in the air as if he were obeying a police order. "You discovered my little secret."

"Oh my god." She turned to run, but Gladson zoomed by her and cut her off.

"I just want to talk to you. We really hit it off, remember? I thought we could bond over work problems."

"What? That's not how that works. Please take me to where I'm supposed to be. I don't want to be late."

"I wouldn't have let you be late. You were right, we did walk in a circle. I apologize. I just," he paused, "I wish you would give me a second chance." He put his left arm on the wall and leaned into it. If Sunny wanted to get by him, her body would have to brush against his.

Sunny bit her cheek, "Please take me to where I'm supposed to be." She released her jaw and touched her tongue to the spot that would disappoint her dentist.

"This way." He motioned with his free arm, not moving from his position.

"You can't lead the way if I'm in front of you." Sunny was not going to move until he did. She thought about Nevasha reporting him, if she should report this. What would she say in the complaint? Creepy hallway posture? Took the long way around?

After a longer pause than needed, Gladson dropped his arm and started walking. "You are a stubborn one, aren't you?" he asked over his shoulder with a smile. "It isn't good to chew your cheeks, and I can smell the infection building."

The room they entered was only three doors down from where they started. It had a fume hood, a vortex, a centrifuge, microplates, blood bank reagents, pens, one marker, downtime resulting cards and a stack of papers. The cover page on the stack read, "Procedure."

"As much as I'd love to stay and give you all the answers. I never understood how people got interested in micro."

"I like micro."

"You'll have to teach me." Gladson stood, not moving.

"Are you allowed to be in here when I start?"

"No." He covered his face with his hands. "Go ahead, I'm not here."

"This is my job. I am being serious."

"You're no fun." Gladson paused in the doorway, "Enjoy your work." An attempt at sarcasm, but Sunny heard the resentment.

Once the room was hers, she opened the packet. "Let's fucking go," she whispered.

The title, "Quality Assurance Unknown."

"There are several laboratory departments you have not been trained in, including microbiology and the blood bank. This week, you will be tested to see if you can follow some of our current procedures. If you do well on the samples today, you will continue with quality assurance training for the rest of the week.

"Not only does this blind sample method test your ability to follow our procedures, it tests our ability to write procedures. Please feel free to mark typos or any other errors you may sea in the margins with red ink."

Sunny noted the red, blue, and black pens sitting in a pen holder with a pencil and a black click-top Sharpie. She also made a mental note to correct "sea" to "see." There was no way she was writing anything before reading this entire packet.

"Enzymes produced by gut bacteria have shown to be effective in the removal of the glycoproteins from the surface of red blood cells.

The removal of N-acetylgalactosamine (A antigen) and D-galactose (B antigen) from donor red blood cells allows donor blood to be transfused to any L-fucose (H antigen) positive donor.

"The H antigen is a precursor to the A and B antigens. Individuals who inherit genes for type A, B, or AB convert the H antigen to their respective blood type. Group O individuals do not convert the H antigen, it remains in it's original state.

"Although rare, individuals with the Bombay phenotype lack the H antigen precursor on the surface of the red blood cells. In testing, they appear to be group O, Rh negative, but they will crossmatch incompatible with O negative blood.

"Antibodies to ABO blood groups develop naturally shortly after birth. Antibodies to other red cell antigens, such as the Rh, Kidd, and Kell groups, can occur after exposure, such as transfusion or pregnancy. These antibodies can also cause incompatible crossmatches and hemolytic transfusion reactions.

"To create a truly universal donor blood, a product that would save countless lives, we must remove all immunogenic glycoproteins from the surface of red blood cells.

"Today, you will extract enzymes from different bacteria to determine which, if any, help achieve our goal of creating a universal blood type."

"Holy shit," Sunny said out loud before she could catch herself. *Be cool, they're watching you. Not cool. Professional. Professionals are cool. Oh my god, focus.*

She read the rest of the packet before investigating her supplies and reagents. A simple enough process. Step one, "Remove bacteria from growth media." They supplied her with three different plates of colony growth: unknown one, unknown two, and unknown three.

Sunny unwrapped a plastic inoculation wand. (A thin, sterile stick with a loop on one side and a hook on the other.) Using the hoop end, she attempted to swipe across the plate without disturbing the gel. Success! She needed to fill a 1.5 milliliter microtube above the 0.5 mL line for each bacterial unknown. After a few sweeps, she zapped the bacteria to the bottom of the tube with a vortex, creating a tightly packed bacteria pellet.

Once she achieved her desired volume, she added a washing solution to each pellet and centrifuged. One milliliter of supernatant from each unknown was transferred to clean, labeled microtubes.

Sunny was also given two segments of blood paired with plasma. Sunny performed forward types on the segments: A pos and B pos. The plasma was type O pos. She performed immediate spin crossmatches with the plasma and each segment. Immediate spin crossmatches are used to determine major ABO compatibility. Two drops of patient plasma, one drop of donor red cells. Sunny noted her findings on her answer sheet.

A pos red cells + O pos plasma = incompatible.

B pos red cells + O pos plasma = incompatible.

She labeled glass tubes with the unknown sample and the blood type. Thirty drops of a four to six percent suspension of red cells plus two drops of each unknown. One additional tube was labeled as an albumin control. Example: Unk 1 + A pos, Unk 2 + A pos, Unk 3 + A pos, and Albumin + Apos. The tubes were placed in a 37 °C heat block and incubated for sixty minutes. She did the same for each unknown and B pos red cells.

As those incubated, Sunny prepped her next set of tubes. When the red cell/bacteria enzyme cook time ended, Sunny repeated her immediate spin crossmatches.

(Unknown One + A pos red cells) + O pos plasma = incompatible.

(Unknown One + B pos red cells) + O pos plasma = incompatible.

As before, these results were concordant with real life.

(Unknown Two + A pos red cells) + O pos plasma = compatible.

"Did I drip something wrong?" She repeated the immediate spin crossmatch and confirmed the same results. "Eeeeeek."

(Unknown Two + B pos red cells) + O pos plasma = incompatible.

Lame.

(Unknown Three + A pos red cells) + O pos plasma = compatible.

Fuck yeah.

(Unknown Three + B pos red cells) + O pos plasma = compatible.

Please let the controls work.

(Albumin + A pos red cells) + O pos plasma = incompatible.

One more to go.

(Albumin + B pos rede cells) + O pos plasma = incompatible.

"That's what I'm talking about." Sunny jumped and pumped her fist into the air.

Ding. Ding. Ding. Ding. Ding.

Sunny screamed and ducked for cover.

A bell rang from a hidden speaker. A voice came from above her. From the ceiling, above the wall closest to the door, dropped a screen. A cartoon sasquatch wearing a labcoat appeared on the projection.

"Amazing. You've successfully engineered universal blood. Unknown three comes directly from the source of our current SBOI. Unknown Two is our manufactured version. As you tested, our version works great with A pos blood, but struggles with cleaning the B pos red cells.

"Vampire gut bacteria, a mutated version of *Akkermansia muciniphila,* are responsible for producing a secretor enzyme that cleaves unwanted antigens from the surface of red blood cells. This super enzyme circulates freely in vampire plasma and saliva, constantly searching for antigens.

"As a field agent, we need you to recognize and flag laboratory test results for vampires. Their complete blood count will have an increased red cell distribution width, with shistocytes and stomatocytes. Blue-green neutrophilic inclusions are a red flag for both vampires and their victims.

"Their blood type will be discrepant. You may find a temporary mixed field in their forward type if they've just fed, most will type as O neg. Their reverse will always type as group AB. Vampires need to feed off living things for hemoglobin, they do not make their own.

Vampires will not feed from animals like horseshoe crabs, which have a copper-based oxygen carrier.

"Because iron is an essential nutrient, vampire gut bacteria evolved their secreter enzyme to prevent any immunoglobulin from destroying their precious red cells prematurely. Thus, vampires are both universal donors and recipients.

"Our researchers, along with special private investors, are working to create a solution to the global blood shortage problem. Relying on donors is both uncertain and risky. Even if everyone who could donate, did, it wouldn't solve the issues of alloantibody development and transfusion reactions. Imagine a world where blood could be created in the lab, free from blood-borne pathogens and immunogenic agents. We need more SBOI volunteers to help make our dream a reality, for the benefit of everyone.

"Please leave your area as is, and someone will be at the door shortly. Congratulations and welcome to the Specialists in Supernatural Beings."

The video stopped, and the screen returned to the ceiling. A knock on the door followed.

"Hey." Nevasha greeted her with a hug.

"Oh, thank god."

"I can't believe they let Gladson bring you here. I told them I needed to follow up with you on something so I could walk you out."

"I can see the lab from here. Why do I need an escort? And, hey, and thank you."

"I can't tell you why," Nevasha pointed up, indicating a security system, "But it's imperative you only walk into the correct rooms." She put her arm around Sunny's shoulders, "Also, I'm going on PTO, so I wanted to tell you now. Please don't forget to say hi when you come back for debriefings or whatever it is you field agents do. No matter what happens out there, remember, you've got a friend in heme."

Sunny laughed. Up to this point, she'd imagined herself going back to Drivers. Until the outbreak, second shift felt like a family. Sunny enjoyed going to work. She wanted to help rebuild that feeling with the new techs. If Felice and the SSB decided she should stay here, with Nevasha, and the badass research on universal blood, it could be home. Heme home.

This was such a good day.

Chapter 19

Current Day

"**What did you learn** from his Facebook page?" Felice asks.

"He had a blue car. People wish him happy birthday every year. He likes to take pictures of nonfiction books. I scrolled pretty far before I saw anything good. By then, I was so tired. I almost missed it."

"By tired, do you mean drunk?"

"It's 0400 in the morning, the library is closed." Ryker snaps her fingers.

"It's 0527."

"Whatever. I mostly stopped because it was the first photo of another person on his profile. A graduation ceremony with the caption, *Congrats sis. Give me a few more years, and I'll be your boss.* The makeup was more Emo Barbie than FDA Inspector Barbie, and she had a septum ring, but it was definitely Eva."

"Siblings? How tragic." Felice says. If she felt anything, her eyes kept it hidden.

Ryker was hitting a wall of full-body awareness. The rise and fall of her chest, her eyelashes touching her puffy eye skin when she blinks, she could feel the hairs on her legs brush against the polyester of her scrub pants. "She was a med tech. Graduated from Texas Tech, same as me, different year."

"Did you share any of this with the police?"

"Of course not. He didn't tell the cops about his sister, why should I?"

"He wrote sis in blood."

"I'm pretty sure that was for me."

Monday: Three Days Ago

THE ALARM CLOCK RADIO crescendoed into NPR, The Texas Standard. Ryker fell in and out of sleep. David Brown interviewed the Chief Science Officer at a Dallas-based biotech company. They performed their first successful pig blood transfusion using semi-artificial universal blood. At 1033 the coffee maker started. At 1036, the coffee maker yelled, and the smell of burning forced Ryker out of bed. It was squeezing leftover droplets of water through yesterday's coffee grounds.

Finding a second dead body at work will throw anyone off their game.

She remembered convincing Last Night Ryker that Morning Ryker would wake up as soon as she heard the radio. Morning Ryker would have plenty of time to prep the machine. Coffee requires exact ratios: one tablespoon of fine dark grounds per six ounces of water.

Filling the water was simple, but she kept losing count with the tablespoons.

His sister. Eva was his sister. He was her brother. Both dead. Dead at Drivers.

She emptied the contents of the cone filter back into its original container. *One, two, three, three murders, four, five, six, sickle cell. Desmund was attacked prior to his exchange. Why didn't he die? Well, die faster?*

Forget starting over a third time. Four more hefty scoops and she hit start.

Ryker felt ridiculous as she typed, but she needed help. "How to solve a murder?"

I don't have time to read a whole book.

"Murder solving process."

Success!

"Every Murder Investigation Uses Four Basic Steps," from Homicide Detectives Inc.

"Step one: Write everything down."

Ryker went to her closet of requirement and retrieved a small purple notebook and pen Liam gave everyone for Lab Week. She wrote down the first step.

"Step two: Everything is evidence."

Out of respect for Andy, Ryker placed Eva's bag back in the corner of Liam's office that night. Out of distrust for authority, she kept its contents. General defiance kept Liam's door open. Fatima didn't lock it, why should Ryker?

The notebook is what led her to Dr. Kudela, a dead end.

She wrote down each item and her initial impression of them in her notebook. The chopsticks are genius. No way Drivers would let her bring a wooden stake inside. Considering the obvious purpose of the stake, the banana and hand sanitizer also had to be vampire-hunting tools.

The hand sanitizer went on in a goopy-to-wet-to-dry manner. Were the ingredients special? Turning the bottle over, something floating in the gel reflected the light shining from the pendants hanging over her breakfast bar. Too early in the morning for big lights, Ryker stepped closer to her balcony window to investigate the object.

Silver. In color, at least, if not real. Shaped like a small pencil. At first glance, she thought it was an earring. In this light, the fastener was wrong. She realized she wasn't the only person to misidentify this object. The same tiny silver accessory lay in Liam's desk drawer.

Add getting that cufflink to my to-do list.

Lotion container in hand, Ryker flipped open the lid like she was ripping into a banana. It smelled like bananas. The little curve in the bottle fit nicely in her palm. It was cute, but was it a weapon? One jarring self-defense item was missing. Wouldn't a vampire hunter have garlic? Her brother was allergic to garlic. If they were a team, it wouldn't make sense to carry around a clove of sibling anaphylactic shock.

"Step three: Map the timeline."

Victim three, Dr. Kudela.

1918: Paged Dr. Kudela.

1944: Dr. Kudela returned page.

2047: Paged again, no response.

2057: Paged Dr. Sanders.

2105: Went to ICU.

2113: Friend Request Notification (didn't see until later).

2132: Wren comes back to lab. Kudela is dead.

If Dr. Kudela approved the friend request, then he died in a nineteen-minute window. That isn't much time for someone to come up to the second floor and leave unnoticed. What was Dr. Kudela doing from 1945 to 2130 that got him killed? Why was he doing all this crystal research? Why the irradiated blood? How does this connect to vampires?

Too many questions. Not enough answers. Fact, Dr. Kudela managed to stay alive, working at Drivers, for six months. His sister killed on day one. Fact, despite being a fraud, the irradiation error that brought her here wasn't planned.

Is that a fact? That was Elyssa's mistake. Could she have done it on purpose? She lives in the same apartment complex as Desmund. Is she part of this?

Second victim, Desmund.

Monday: First attack, didn't die. Why?

Thursday: Left AMA, dead.

The only way for Ryker to know the actual time he left AMA is to look in his chart. HIPAA violations on deceased patients who've been on the news is a quick way to get fired.

Flipping to a fresh page, Ryker wrote, "Eva's timeline."

Thanks to Fatima's constant updates from that day, Eva's movements were well documented. "If you need me, I'll be with Eva, the FDA inspector doing X."

During the inspection, Ryker chalked it up to Fatima's overbearing sense of self-importance. Maybe she was setting Eva up on a silver platter? Informing the vampire of her movements so they could strike her down at the opportune moment. Or...

"Step four: Every lead is worth following."

Could Fatima be the vampire? Is that why she's trying to make me feel crazy? To throw me off my game? Slow down. Let's get back to the timeline.

Nope. She doesn't get emails at home. Who could've guessed maintaining an electronic boundary would inhibit her from solving murders? Deep breath. She'd have to fill that in later. Ryker gazed at the lotion while she opened a real banana and took a bite. *Sweet mushy potassium.* A thought rushed into her head. She started typing before she swallowed, "Does garlic have potassium?"

Not a ton. Twelve milligrams per clove. Bananas contain four hundred twenty. People aren't throwing one clove of garlic at vampires. They're hanging whole wreaths of it over doors. Twelve milligrams times ten cloves per garlic head times ten heads in a wreath, that's over a thousand milligrams of potassium.

I always thought it was the smell that repelled vampires. They weren't eating all that garlic. Maybe they didn't know enough about garlic or potassium back when all these vampire stories started taking place? If vampires come from people, then they know as much about science as people. If I'm an old, dumb vampire, and I drink blood that hurts me, and that person had garlic breath, I might think the garlic hurts me. Now I'm scared of garlic. I tell my old dumb vampire buddies garlic hurts us, like real bad. Now they're scared of garlic. Enough people believe a conspiracy theory, it becomes lore.

Oh fuck. I know what Dr. Kudela was doing with the irradiated blood.

NEXT TO THE SHIFT report was a sign-up sheet for people to pledge their attendance to the Thanksgiving Dinner. Departments with a sixty percent pledge rate and a ninety percent attendance of pledges would receive Drivers-branded water bottles. The only people listed were Malia and Elyssa.

First on Ryker's list of suspects, Fatima. Other than Elyssa's claim that Fatima wouldn't have had time to kill Eva, Fatima fit into every timeline. Maybe her slow waddle was a ruse, or how she preferred to move when she wasn't in vampire mode. Like how Kangaroos take slow weird steps with their tail instead of hopping everywhere to conserve energy. Plus, the way she'd been trying to blame Ryker for all the lab's problems, it had to be some sort of mind trick. A distraction to prevent Ryker from seeing the truth.

"Ryker, I appreciate you trying to save me time, but I have no problems for you today."

Was that humor? Stick to the plan. Quick, before it dries.

"Did I leave my pen in here the other day?" she asked. "It's similar to this one." Ryker motioned with her hand towards the black plastic holder on the edge of Fatima's desk. "Oh, I'm so sorry," she said as it plummeted to the floor.

Her acting was terrible, but it worked. Fatima hobbled over to help Ryker pick the pens, pencils, and highlighters up off the floor. As Fatima reached for her holder, Ryker also reached for it, ensuring their hands touched.

Fatima pulled her hand away, disgust and annoyance not hidden on her face. "Is that sweat? Ryker, are you ill? I don't know what special pen you have, Ryker, but it's not in my office."

"You're right, I'm sorry." She used the desk to help herself stand. Fatima was giving her a cold, hard stare. "I'm not sick. It's hand sanitizer. I always pump after I sign in. Guess it was extra goopy today."

"So I don't need to file a blood and body fluid exposure form?" Fatima laughed.

"No, but I expect that pen holder to be secure for sea on my next inspection."

They shared a laugh this time.

"Thank you, Ryker, my days are always more interesting when I speak with you."

Either the hand sanitizer didn't work, or Fatima wasn't a vampire. Worse than that, this might have helped them bond a little.

Next on her list, and her way around the lab, Liam. Not bothering with words, she walked in, took a piece of candy out of his bowl, palmed it into a dot of sanitizer, and gave it back to him. He held it for a few moments before he spoke.

"I don't understand what's happening."

Ryker waited in silence for the vampire chemicals to work their magic.

"Do you want me to make a different kind? Dr. Sanders seems to be the only one who enjoys the Diet Coke flavor."

"Dr. Pepper, please," Ryker said, assuming it had been long enough. Liam wasn't her vampire either. "Full strength."

"I'm going to assume you mean I have not completed the annual competency packet, thus maintaining the CAP requirements to perform bench tech laboratory functions?" He raised his eyebrows.

Ryker shrugged.

"I was a tech for seventeen years. All morning I worked with Malia. I was signed off on receiving specimens and blood products, and loading and answering type and screens from the machine. There is no sign-off for answering the phones."

"What about issuing blood?"

"Yvette will be here."

The irony of having a hero dinner and mandating employees to come because they've been deemed non-essential.

"I got written up for scanning samples instead of helping Ryker with an MTP," said June. "Now you're saying that's what your job will be."

Rewind to a couple weeks after June started full-time. Ryker was in the middle of preparing the third shipment on an MTP for Labor and Delivery when another MTP order came in from the ICU. June skipped over the order on the printer to find a type and screen order she was receiving. Ryker mentioned it to Yvette out of frustration. Yvette, as a new supervisor, made it an official complaint. June was still butthurt.

"These are different circumstances," said Liam.

"How? If there's an MTP, what will you do? Get ice? Can you thaw plasma? Not even an MTP. What if NICU orders a syringe for a baby at the same time OR comes to pick up blood and tissues? I was told we are all responsible for prioritizing patient care." June's face flushed with anger.

"We thought through as many scenarios as possible..." Liam was cut off.

"This is how people die." Elyssa's hand was shaking, her eyes red. "You expect us to sit in the cafeteria, listening to their bullshit about how we are honoring the memories of loved ones. Meanwhile, up here, you're adding more patients to the death list?"

Vampire calling the kettle black.

"Elyssa, didn't you sign the pledge sheet? You were already going to the dinner?" Yvette asked.

Bet she planned on making a dinner out of the ICU. Now we'll be there watching her.

"I thought if I went, other people would stay up here," Elyssa said.

"We hear your concerns," Liam continued. "This is the best solution we have for the circumstances."

"Please have the volume turned up on your phones." Yvette exchanged a stare with Ryker, which meant she disagreed with this solution, but she lost the battle. "I will be calling you if we have an MTP."

Ryker, June, and Elyssa shared annoyed, but silent head shakes of defeat.

Two hours before they had to go to the cafeteria. The mandatory dinner wasn't part of her vampire exposure plan, but she could make it work.

"I have a wibit!" June shouted from the centrifuges.

Fatima, on her way towards the exit, reversed.

"What's a wibit?" Quinneth dried her hands.

"Wrong blood in tube," June said as she held out the specimen. A four-milliliter lavender top had been labeled correctly as a CBC, but another label adhered over it contained nothing but computer gibberish. It appeared as if the name, MRN, and DOB were typed in Wingdings.

"Oh, no," Quinneth smiled, "That's just how the label printed."

"You put this label on this specimen?" Fatima asked.

"Yeah, I don't know why it printed that way. It's a confirm type," Quinneth said.

"If a sample came from the floor like this, it would be rejected. Why would you give me this to run? Are you trying to set me up?" She paced as she spoke. June's short stature could not contain her fury.

"Please, please." Fatima held up her hands. "Is there a blood order for that sample?"

"No." June added, "Unless Quinneth didn't match the blood order to the confirm type."

Ryker pressed her lips together to hide her smile as she flipped through the pending orders, "There's no blood order."

"June, please make me a photocopy. Go ahead and cancel the tests on this sample and order another confirm type. Quinneth, please come to my office so we can finish this discussion." Fatima continued mumbling to herself as Quinneth followed. Caught in the act, with witnesses. Management will finally have to deal with her incompetence.

The anticipation of outing a vampire was building in her mind. The tension at the table, the gotcha moment. Ryker needed a distraction. No one wants to be in the hospital on a normal night. Around Thanksgiving, people tend to avoid addressing their ailments until after the holiday. Which is probably why Yvette thought she could handle the lab with just her and Liam for two hours. A tinge of guilt tasted like acid reflux in the back of her throat. *Maybe we were too reactive to going to dinner? I'll ask Yvette if she wants me to bring her a to-go plate.*

"Code blue, Drivers Hospital, fifteenth floor, room 153."

She turned to manual, Elyssa was gone. If she was sneaking a early dinner, Ryker needed to act. Now. She ripped off her gloves and labcoat. "June, I'll be right back." She called out as she opened the door.

Ooooof. She collided with Elyssa's shoulder, almost knocking her down. Elyssa changed her shirt. Or added a shirt to it. When the shift started, she was wearing a teal scrub top; now she had a sweater over it. *Hiding the blood from the ICU?*

"Sorry," Elyssa said as she regained her balance. "I'm here now, I can help cover desk."

"How do you know desk needs help. Where'd you go?" Ryker's eyes narrowed.

"I went to the bathroom, I heard the code blue over the speakers." Elyssa ducked around Ryker into the lab.

"You need a sweater to go to the bathroom?" Ryker released her foot from the door.

"I'm cold."

"I bet." Ryker went back to her workstation. She wasn't going to let Elyssa out of her sight for the rest of the night. No blood orders for the code blue. It was obvious Elyssa had no plans on stopping. Sucking the lives out of patients and employees and fraud visitors one at a time. Patient safety is Ryker's number one priority. That meant Elyssa had to die. Tonight.

"DID YOU BUY THAT at the gift shop?" June tugged on the sleeve of Elyssa's purple Drivers sweatshirt. "It looks comfortable. Like you have plenty of room in there to hide some to go turkey."

Elyssa laughed, "I like to wear oversized."

June held open the stairwell door. "I don't want to go first, just in case," she smiled.

Employees and guests meandered throughout the first-floor atrium. 1657, three minutes until the official start time.

"How's it going being straight?" A voice asked behind Ryker.

"Sunny!" Ryker burst with excitement. "I didn't know you were coming."

"How could I resist that invitation? Plus, I expedited my re-start date to Monday. We'll be work buddies again next week!"

Ryker's excitement shifted into suspicion. Felice laughed at her when she mentioned vampires. Now that there's one more dead body, they're sending Sunny back early? How much did the SSB know?

A small crowd bottlenecked at the cafeteria entrance. A multicolored balloon arch served as the starting point for the line. Golden yellow, red, white, and a scattering of purple balloons formed a semicircle of inflatable wild corn. Each purple balloon embellished with the Drivers logo. On either side of the arch sat bales of hay with purple painted pumpkins. Employees, the business casual pants with a purple themed T-shirt pegged them as admin, wore novelty turkey headpieces as they greeted diners and directed them to the meal service lines.

"You doing, ok?" June asked, patting Elyssa on the shoulder.

Her nervous energy read like a marquee sign. She kept her gaze low. Avoiding all eye contact. "It's a bit much."

"All these blood-pumping-meat-sacks overwhelming your senses?" asked Ryker.

"That's the weirdest way possible to put it, but yes. Plus, the colors. And what the hell is this music?" Elyssa clasped her hands and rubbed her thumb into her palm.

Far from Linda Belcher's "Pass the Cranberry Sauce," Drivers found a random Thanksgiving playlist. They walked into an upbeat James Brown's "Do the Mash Potato." Now "Thank U," by Alanis Morrissette, shoved its depressing melody down their eardrums.

"Turkey trot to the left," the line monitor beckoned June and Elyssa.

"Gobble gobble to the right," another directed Ryker and Sunny.

Did she plan on outing Elyssa as a vampire during dinner? Yes. Was she going to do it on an empty stomach? No. However, she couldn't hide the disapproval on her face from the people serving food. The ill-fitted gloves, the falling off hair nets, haphazardly tied aprons, and themed t-shirts suggested they were also from admin. An offensive cosplay of nutrition services.

"Why the long face?"

Why the long hair? Technically, she was wearing a hair net. Her waist-length hair was pulled back with a small clip and slung over the front of her shoulder, dangling inches away from the turkey. The gravy was supposed to be optional. The man with chin hairs sticking out on all sides of his beard net wasn't pausing long enough between asking, "Gravy?" and sloping it onto the plate. Though neon green might not be a traditional gravy color, Ryker enjoyed the taste. She'd had it every year since she started at Drivers. Despite the rumors surrounding the origin of its color, it's never caused an outbreak.

The green beans were an absolute no. They tasted like Drivers canned and froze the leftovers every year, then microwaved them in plastic to serve again. Not even the gravy could help them. Last, there were bread rolls and pie. A choice between sweet potato or pecan. Whatever hell Drivers put the green beans through, the sweet potato pie received the opposite. Crispy buttery crust, dense, brown sugar sweet potato filling, embellished with flame-melted marshmallows.

"What are you really doing here?" Realizing how rough it sounded, Ryker tried again. "I mean, I'm very happy to see you. I called Felice last week, and now you're back the day before a holiday."

Sunny laughed, "I wanted to spend Thanksgiving with my family."

"I thought all your family was in Oklahoma?" Too many things were floating around Ryker's head for her to keep obvious questions inside.

"My work family," Sunny winked.

Ryker grunted.

"What? You love us. Me, June, Yvette, and now we have an Elyssa baby," she elbowed Ryker in the side.

"There's something I need to tell you about her."

Too late, they reached the table. Sunny greeted everyone with another big smile, "Happy Thanksgiving."

They sat through Ariana Grande's "Thank U, Next." Elyssa poked at her food. Small children do a better job at pretending to eat vegetables than she did with a full tray of fall fare.

"Too much garlic?" Ryker asked.

"Garlic, salt, green, I'm not in the mood for any of this," Elyssa replied.

Ryker leaned in closer, "I know who you are."

"Really?" Elyssa's eyes squinted. "I didn't tell anyone. How did you figure it out?"

"The timeline mostly, and the silver." Ryker expected her to put up more of a fight.

Elyssa looked at her left hand, the same hand that burned on the computer mouse.

"I didn't think anyone noticed. Is it ok?" Elyssa's eyes glazed over with tears.

"Ok? How could this be ok?" When she prepped for this confrontation in her head, there was never a moment when Elyssa would ask for forgiveness.

"I, I thought we were friends. I thought if I could fit in, then tell you, it wouldn't be so awkward."

Awkward? You're a vampire, not a quirky girl next door.

"I don't think that's possible. You don't belong here. You're hurting people. You're hurting our patients." This conversation was too confusing to maintain the intense level of anger she prepared. Why would Elyssa think Ryker would be ok with her feeding from and killing patients? There's got to be some other way to survive without murder. "We work in a blood bank. Can't you get your fix without draining everyone?"

"I didn't realize I was such a burden." Slow tears fell down Elyssa's cheek.

The weeping, the chattering in the background, Sister Sledge's "We are Family," it was too much to process. Ryker froze. She did not expect to feel bad for telling someone they can't eat people.

"The ceremony is about to begin." The gobble to the right woman said into a microphone. She didn't add, "This is the mandatory part," but the quieting of the audience suggested they picked up what she was putting down.

The Drivers CEO walked towards an ill-placed podium. In stark contrast to the business slacks and skirts worn by his brethren, he sported a pair of faded dad jeans and old tennis shoes with his T-shirt. He's not like other CEO's, he's a cool CEO. The eighty-six-inch flat screen tv on the ceiling updated its display from the official dinner invitation to a PowerPoint.

"Welcome, friends and family, to our Drivers Thanksgiving Memorial and Hero Dinner." The people in themed shirts led a flaccid applause. "Today, we want to celebrate the heroes who kept Drivers going during our most trying time, while honoring the memories of those who cannot be here with us. We don't have time to share every story, and believe me, I wish we did. Every single employee deserves recognition for their heroic actions during an unprecedented time."

Brain splatter. A wrench. Splat. A steel pole. Splat. A broom. The knot in Ryker's shoulder tensed.

"We want to share a video capturing the stories of a few whose deeds inspired us to update our Drivers core values. Drivers is more than a workplace, it's a calling. Our new core values represent those people who answered the call: courage, unity, neighborliness, trust, safety."

The flat screen he read from, updated with the first letter of each new core value capitalized, bolded, and underlined. "C U N T S." Crowd reactions ranged from gasps to giggles as the letters started spinning for further emphasis.

"I apologize to everyone here." The CEO's face turned bright red. "Will someone please stop that video?"

Panic set in amongst the administration representatives. They formed a huddle. Whispers, finger pointing, eye rolls. All to end with the selected representative shaking their head at the CEO.

"It appears someone with poor taste thought this would be funny. Allow me a moment to pull up our genuine new core values."

The screen went black.

"Thank you to whoever managed to turn the television off."

The Netflix theme noise blasted through the speakers. Something moved on the black screen. It started small and out of focus. It grew until the Pi symbol covered the entire screen. The crowd went completely silent.

Bold yellow words started from the bottom of the screen and scrolled on a tilted axis, growing smaller as they approached the top. "On a night not long ago, in the territory known as Drivers, an outbreak decimated the city. Citizens were told it was an accident, but a few vigilant rebels discovered the truth. In a move to restore order, leadership hastened to replace the victims of their evil deed with corporate CUNTS. Tonight, the rebels honor those who died due to the malice and greed of the Drivers Regime..."

The in memoriam video that followed featured a person's name, department, years of service to Drivers, and a series of personal photos. No more jokes. Real photos of people lost. A man at the table next to Ryker's started clapping for each name that appeared on the screen. Soon, the entire cafeteria filled with applause.

The CEO stood dumbfounded at the podium. Interrupting the video now would be far more disrespectful than the fake core values. Ryker wondered how horrible the real video must have been for the Pi Rats to risk their jobs over a tactful remembrance.

"Scott Burkhardt, Transfusion Services, six years." Applause. The first photo was a full headshot of a big smile through a bigger beard. The second was professional. Scott on one knee with the sunlight in the background, giving him and his fiancée a dark silhouette against the pink and orange Texas sky. Ryker felt sick. The third was another engagement photo. Scott and his fiancée sitting in front of a row of hedges, blooming with white hydrangeas.

Oh fuck. Ooooooh fuck. I fucked. I fucked so bad.

The names continued in alphabetical order.

"Elyssa," Ryker whispered. "I didn't know. I promise I didn't know."

Quiet tears rolled down Elyssa's face.

"Ryker, what did you do?" Sunny scolded.

"She told me the truth," Elyssa said.

"Ryker does not speak for us." June held her hand across the table for Elyssa to hold. Elyssa sat on her hands, keeping her head down.

"You guys liked Scott." Tears fell into her lap.

Ryker, Sunny, and June shrugged in silence.

"Yeah, we all did." Sunny couldn't hide the distaste that came with lying.

Elyssa lifted her head before Sunny could reset.

"Wait, why else would Ryker tell me I didn't belong here?"

All eyes on her, Ryker had to confess. "I thought you were a vampire," she paused. "In the spirit of honesty, being engaged to Scott doesn't make that impossible."

Elyssa let out a short, inappropriate burst of laughter. "Why the hell would a vampire fall in love with Scott?" she asked.

The people at the tables near them shushed Elyssa's volume.

Ryker didn't have a good answer. "It takes a lot of blood to move around a body that size?"

The table smothered their snickering.

"I'm not a vampire. I'm an asshole. Scott and I met in college. I broke up with him the night before the outbreak. He told me about mistyping those cords. Then he tried to make an excuse for why it was ok. I said I couldn't marry someone who didn't take accountability for their actions." She wiped tears from her eyes. "He text me a photo of his certificate for Laboratorian of the Quarter after the staff meeting. I told him two wrongs don't make a right."

"Ouch," Sunny said, "If it helps you feel better, we all thought the same thing."

"His parents never knew I left him. I didn't know how to talk to anyone about it after the funeral. For a while, I wanted to disappear. Start over with a new life. That felt like running away from my problems. I started with a new apartment. Then I thought about you guys. He said he was tired of y'all writing him up. I told him to stop making so many mistakes. That's why I came here. I thought, of all the people, second shift would understand. The original memorial video had a feature on Scott. On how wonderful he was as a tech. A quiet leader in the blood bank. I couldn't stomach watching." Her face saddened.

The screen faded, the crowd gave a standing ovation. A group of a dozen people in purple Drivers sweatshirts and matching masquerade masks remained standing after the crowd. Even with their Superman level disguises, Ryker recognized Malia, the jerk from the STAT lab, Officer Russel, and parking lot Karen.

"This is the part I never agreed with." Elyssa nodded towards the group gathering near the podium.

After a few moments, words reappeared on the screen, "The CUNTS who benefited from your pain." The video started with the same photo as the in memoriam, the smiling short-haired, older woman faded into a youthful blonde. Her name, job title, promotion date, and unqualified written underneath. A high-pitched squeal came from the table to the left of Ryker.

"I didn't do anything wrong. Jean was my mentor. I went to her funeral." The blond NICU charge nurse stormed towards the balloon arch exit.

Marco's picture appeared on the screen, then faded to Yvette, "Unqualified."

"Fuck you, Malia," Ryker screamed over the Golden Girls theme song. Prior to the outbreak, Drivers required six months as a senior tech before someone was eligible to be a supervisor. Second shift lost her, too. They updated the requirement to one year as a lead tech. Malia was more bitter than Ryker's morning coffee. Yvette had five years as lead and a total of nine years at Drivers. She was hands down the most experienced bench tech in Drivers blood bank.

The thing about inciting a riot, you should probably do it on purpose. Ryker did not plan on throwing a dinner roll covered in gravy at Malia's head. She definitely didn't plan on Sunny, June, and Elyssa following her example. There's no way she could have planned the blond nurse running back with a tray of mashed potatoes and tossing them onto parking lot Karen. Or that leading to a full-on food fight.

Officer Russel took a slung hunk of turkey to his left cheek. Green beans made great projectiles. Noticeably missing from the fight were the pie slices. Admin ran to guard the remaining trays of turkey, gravy, and rolls with the CEO hiding behind them, shouting, "We have names and ID numbers. This is not a representation of our values."

"Time to go," Ryker said.

Elyssa wiped a handful of mashed potatoes off her face. "The garlic," she said as she fainted.

"What?" Ryker screamed.

Elyssa stood up, laughing, and licked the potatoes off her finger. "It could use way more garlic."

On their way out, the sign-in sheet, which the CEO just mentioned, sat unaccompanied on a table near the balloon arch. In one smooth motion, Ryker swiped the clipboard and tucked it under her arm.

Chapter 21

SLIDE ONE, "VAMPIRE: A Drivers Case Study."

Slide two, "In today's lesson, you will learn: (1) Evidence supporting the presence of a vampire at Drivers (2) Emerging theories in clinical vampire science (3) Which one of you is a killer."

Slide three, "The evidence. Victim one admitted Monday, November 17th after being attacked by, in his words, a demon. Blue-green crystals appeared in his peripheral blood smear that same day. Unfortunately, this would not be the last time this poor soul faced his callous foe."

Slide four, "Victim two." Sunny extended the pointer in her hand and whipped the wall behind her. "Wednesday, November 19th, under the guise of an FDA inspector, the unidentified vampire huntress arrived at Drivers at 1000 and departed this mortal coil around 1700. Her skin went from a vibrant caramel to a pale oat milk. Two small puncture wounds noted on her neck." Sunny pressed two fingers into her neck, demonstrating the location. "Found in her bag was a notebook with the names of several Drivers patients written. Each of those patients had Death Crystals in their blood. All died a day later, except one."

Slide five, "Victim one, again, and for the final time. Left Drivers AMA at an unknown time because his chart is behind the glass. We do not break the glass, people." Sunny delivered this line as if she were prepping a war room. "Thursday around 1630, his body was ripped to pieces, not by a demon or a dog, no, this was a vampire."

Slide six, "Victim three." Sunny paused, titling her head towards the ground for a somber moment. "The brother of the vampire huntress and current Blood Bank resident. He'd been writing a paper on the crystals, studying these patients. Did he find a cure? A way to stop the vampire transformation? Murdered. Sunday, November 23rd. His body left in a dramatic slump. The same bite mark on his neck. Message received, vampire."

Sunny held up her hand, "Please hold all applause for the end."

Slide seven, "Modern vampire theories. Why the crystals? Vampire bites leave a calling card. The act of removing such a high volume of blood within a short period creates a sudden drop in the body's oxygenation. This induces a sudden state of lactic acidosis, which forms the crystals. Plenty of techs have seen a sudden appearance of death crystals, not all are vampire bites. However, the addition of stomatocytes is key to this identification process.

"We've shown vampire enzymes can," Sunny cleared her throat and restarted. "We hypothesize there is an enzyme secreted in vampire saliva that removes any surface-level antigens from red blood cells, thus making any blood type a yummy option. Stomatocytes are associated with alcoholism and liver disease. They are also associated with the legendary Rh null phenotype. We believe when the vampire bites, like the snake delivers its venom, the vampire releases this enzyme into its victim. Essentially, meal prepping for its return."

Slide eight, "Why irradiated blood? Red blood cells are hardy little worker bees. One irradiation cycle and their membranes become weak. We suspect when the vampire enzyme goes to town on an irradiated cell, the membrane collapses. If vampires are sensitive to sunlight, and if the irradiator used UV rays, we would be transfusing microscopic grenades waiting for the enzyme to remove their pin. Alas, the sunlight thing is still up for debate, and we use X-rays. Which, if vampires were sensitive to X-rays, there would be more than one documented case of sudden human combustion during CT scans.

"What happens when red cells burst? They release potassium. While it's on the same column as sodium, the extra potassium doesn't taste like French fries. It's gross, probably, and more importantly, it causes hyperkalemia. Stomachache, diarrhea, and vomiting are not suitable for vampire lifestyles. Fun fact, another food high in potassium, bananas. Or, an entire head of garlic. Much like a wreath of garlic on your door wards vampires away from your home, Dr. Kudela discovered the extra potassium from the internally hemolyzed irradiated blood warded off the vampire enzyme and thus the vampire transformation."

Slide nine, "The timeline. You are all here because you had both means and opportunity for the last three known vampire murders at Drivers."

Sunny paced around the table.

"You, Liam, hated the idea of failing your first FDA inspection."

"Or was it you, Fatima?" Sunny jumped into a lunge and pointed her finger. "You also hated the idea of failing an inspection. Plus, you've been gaslighting Ryker, trying to throw her off your scent. Even vampires can reek of bullshit.

"Perhaps it was Quinneth? Eva kept nagging you, asking you to do your job. How dare she?

"One of you stalked the agent into the bathroom with the intent to kill her before she could submit her report. That's when you discovered she knew your identity, and you were glad you had already decided to kill her."

"Each of you has been given a swab. You will wipe the outer side of your gums, under your lips. We will test known AB positive blood with a four percent solution made of regular blood bank saline. Then, we will test in saline mixed with your swabs. Whichever blood comes out as O negative, that's our vampire, and our murderer."

Sunny hit the lights. She made sure to deep clean her kitchen and hide all the moving boxes before this video conference.

"Congratulations, Sunny. This presentation not only exposes you as an SSB agent, it gives away top secret information regarding the vampire enzyme. We're this close to FDA approval for our universal blood, and you'd screw all that up, risk all those potential lives saved, for what? Catching a single vampire?" Even through a laptop camera, Felice was scary as hell. "How did you plan on getting them all in the conference room?"

"Ryker thought..."

"There's your problem, Ryker isn't in the SSB, Sunny is. Say Ryker can get them in there, how did you plan on forcing them to cooperate with the swabs? You call me saying you need a midnight meeting, and this is what you present?" The vignette around Felice darkened with every word.

Sunny bit the inside of her cheek, "I thought it was a good plan."

"You'd be better off putting garlic powder in the water towers." Felice rubbed her forehead.

"That's it!" Sunny squealed.

Felice didn't startle. The longer Sunny proposed her new plan, the softer her stare became. At the end, she nearly smiled.

Chapter 22

Current Day

"**THAT'S IT?**" **LIGHT GLISTENS** ever so gently off the center of Felice's forehead, her chin, too. "One bite of mashed potatoes and you no longer think she's a vampire?"

"There was more," Ryker says, sounding as defensive as possible. "During Scott's funeral and the planning, Elyssa didn't know what to do. She felt so guilty. To avoid picking the skin off her fingertips, she sat on her hands. Gave herself an ulcer. The silver in the hand sanitizer counteracted with her prescription lotion. Which I verified with the package insert."

"What about not eating cake or pizza? Wasn't that your biggest piece of evidence?"

"Oh yeah, turns out she just doesn't want to eat that stuff."

"And you're ok with that?" Felice asks.

"Am I ok with getting an extra portion of food? It's like you don't even know me."

"After the dinner, you and Sunny, I'm assuming mostly you, came up with that halfcocked scheme."

"Flattery will get you nowhere. That plan was, at best, loose sausage meat. Starting a food fight is exhilarating. Like when someone takes your shirt off for the first time and grunts when they see what you have to offer. That kind of adrenaline fills you with more confidence than logic."

Flirting with the head of a secret agency while being interrogated was almost equally exciting. At this point in the night, making bedroom eyes kept things interesting. It added a level of danger to the cat-and-mouse game. Felice was such a strong, powerful woman.

Wednesday: One Day Ago

SIX PEOPLE IN BLACK scrubs loitered at the employee entrance. A greeter at the doors directed everyone to the person with the sign-in sheet. Four blood drawing stations lined and blocked the sliding glass exit doors.

"We're with the CDC. We received an email last night implicating the dinner gravy in another outbreak. As a precaution, we are taking samples from all employees upon arrival," the greeter said.

"What about the guests?" Elyssa asked as she showed her badge to the man at the sign-in sheet.

"We are doing our best to make house calls. The list of attendees vanished during the commotion." The greeter repositioned herself to redirect another employee.

"You guys already got me today," Dr. Sanders said without slowing his stride. The greeter, a tall woman with Brienne of Tarth energy, held up her hand. "Please wait a moment while we verify."

He produced his badge and tapped his foot as he waited.

"Thank you for your participation, Dr. Sanders," she stepped aside.

"You didn't give me a choice, did you?" He smiled at Elyssa and Ryker, "I'll let Liam know you're held up here, and not to charge you any tardies. We've got another meeting today."

Elyssa held the cotton swab down as the phlebotomist applied her band-aid. "Everything ok, Ryker? You're suspiciously compliant."

Ryker checked her phone. This wasn't the plan. Sunny wasn't responding to her texts.

"Still recharging my insolence." Ryker lifted her coffee tumbler. "I donate blood at ABI all the time. Giving a purple top to a stranger isn't much different. You did a great job on that, by the way." Ryker said to the phlebotomist.

"Thanks. Your vein sits right on top of your tendon. I can see how that might be painful sometimes," he replied.

"That's the good one, too. I've yelped when new phlebs try the other arm."

"You let them draw you from a place you know will hurt?" Elyssa asked.

"Yeah. But. It's a good lesson. They need to listen to people when they're giving them advice about their bodies." Ryker stood.

"Real quick," the phlebotomist said. "Are the screams on purpose?"

"No. It's genuine pain. We all get scared," Ryker said, nodding to Elyssa. "You ready?"

As promised, Dr. Sanders was waiting in the lab, Liam at his side.

"Ryker, you're always the last one here for our get-togethers," Dr. Sanders glanced at Elyssa who apparently goes directly to the lab after clocking in. Ryker did her usual. Standing in the breakroom, sipping her coffee for a couple minutes, building courage.

"Yes, well, I'm the first to annoy you with questions," she said with a small salute.

Dr. Sanders laughed, "First shift has been dealing with this all day. The blood samples the CDC drew upon entrance are getting a complete blood count and a forward ABORh only. They would not give me any clinical evidence to support their claims. They said the types were mandatory to eliminate any ABO specificity with the alleged infectious agent, and red cell testing alone would be sufficient."

"What that means for you," Liam continued. "The STAT lab will be running the CBCs, then a designated volunteer will walk the completed samples to the blood bank for ABO testing. Any questions? Ryker?" Liam added that last part before she raised her hand.

"What kind of labels do they have? I'm assuming we have to manually program them on the machines? Are we printing the results, or are they going to come with a flash drive or something later? What if there is an ABO discrepancy? Are we working those up?" That was enough to start.

"Forward types only. A discrepancy would mean we verified ABO concordance with a reverse type." Liam raised his eyebrows. "If you meant non-determinant types, all results are once and done. Everything is accepted as is, including any question marks. Samples are blind, with a barcode and no other identifying information. Yes, they need to be manually programmed. You are not to print any results. Someone will be in tomorrow morning to download those files." Liam paused. "Yvette has PTO today. Ryker, you're lead tonight. Anything else?"

"Where are we storing them?" Elyssa asked.

"I don't know," Liam said. "Fatima, where has first shift been storing the CDC samples?"

Fatima's eyes circled between her techs.

Quinneth raised her hand chest high, "We have lots of empty storage racks we could use."

"I will make sure they are all together. I will put them on the investigation shelf in the fridge." Fatima scurried off.

"How's it going, Ryker?" Malia asked through a fake smile.

"Pretty good, I had a great meal last night. How are you?" Ryker didn't bother smiling. It was too early for that nonsense. "Not wearing your pin today?

"I have no idea what you're talking about." Malia placed a sample on the counter with a half-completed antibody ID sheet. "The only thing pending is a full phenotype for a new dara patient."

Only a fool would jump into testing based on the history check and turnover from first shift. Their desk techs only care about the bare minimum: previous type, antibodies, or special instructions. For no reason at all, their manual techs assume the person on desk has done a thorough dive into the chart. "I trust my coworkers." The bullshit line they use to maintain minimum effort and accountability.

A few clicks in SAGA and Ryker discovered the patient was transfused a month ago at another facility. A phenotype tests the antigens on the surface of red blood cells. Transfused red blood cells circulate in the recipient's body for around ninety days. During this time, the donor blood can interfere with a phenotype and cause incorrect or inconclusive results. Her one pending sample turned into a send-out for molecular testing.

Everyone left by 1530, including Liam. Fatima did a half ass job of collecting the CBC samples. Unless there were only a handful of people working at Drivers that day. The rest of the completed samples were located in a mixture of the regular storage racks, on the analyzers, and sprinkled through the workstations. Still, the volume was low.

"Hey, sis," Andy answered.

"Are you testing the CBCs for the employees? We're running types, but the numbers aren't adding up."

"Yes, I can help you with that. Do you have the medical record number?" Then Andy whispered, "We're only sending you the ones with a specific RDW or higher. Do you have any idea what this is about?"

"The thing you didn't want to be involved in."

"Yes, that sample resulted ten minutes ago. Have you tried hitting refresh on your screen?" Then he added, "Whatever you're doing, stay safe."

"Thanks, fam." Ryker hung up.

Information from Andy explained the low volume of testing coming from the STAT lab. It also made Ryker think about Desmund. When he showed up to Drivers, the first time, it was his RDW that threw the first blood bank red flag. Red blood cell distribution width, RDW, measures the variance in the size of red blood cells. A healthy person, with only their own blood in their veins (not recently transfused), will have an RDW between eleven to fifteen percent. Those with someone else's blood in their circulation will most likely have a higher RDW.

Why would the SSB care about employees who got transfusions?

The answer hit her brain like a Mentos in Diet Coke.

Vampires drink other people's blood. It's not exactly FDA-approved, but it is a type of transfusion. They would have to have a high

RDW. Certainly, after drinking the blood of at least three people in one week.

One of these samples belongs to our vampire. Sunny's a fucking genius.

She wouldn't tell Ryker what, but the SSB must have a way to test for vampirism. Sunny wanted to gather all the suspects in one room. There's no reason to do that if your only plan was to throw garlic and silver spoons at people until they freaked out and bared their fangs.

"Transfusion this is Ryker...Why did you request blood if you don't have the patient...that is not an option...The provider does not the authority to tell me how to issue blood products...Send it back to the blood bank, if it is out of temp we will have to waste it...It does, thanks."

"June," Ryker said after hanging up with the unit clerk. "ER is sending back a unit of blood. The patient somehow went to the OR in the time between ER asking for the blood and them receiving it."

"What did the provider not have the authority to tell you?" Elyssa asked.

"He claimed it was already issued to the patient, so we can send it over to the OR once it comes back from the ED."

A hefty carrier thunked in the tube station. June took its temperature, "9.8!"

Blood products have a transport requirement of one to ten degrees Celsius. The unit would be spared an early death.

Ryker called the ER, "Hey, we got the unit. It's still in temp. We don't have to discard it."

"Oh my god," the unit clerk cheered. "Thank you so much for letting me know. I was going to be worrying about that all night. I would've felt so bad if an O neg got thrown away. I hope you have a great night."

The agony of exclusion from Sunny's plan taunted Ryker's thoughts. With no work to distract her, she reached for a discarded order in the shred bin. She needed to slow her mind. Without a specific design intention, she placed her pencil at the edge of a pipette tip box and traced the square onto her sheet. Starting at the edge, she dragged the graphite in random directions. Once the shapes and spaces achieved a pretty balance, she darkened the lines with a black marker, rounding the intersections. Allowing her mind to smooth out as she smoothed out the corners.

Reusing HIPAA paper relieved the stress of making a good drawing. At the end of the night, the page went into the shred bin no matter the outcome. Occasionally, she would sketch something more fun. If it was worth keeping, she'd make a photocopy to keep the art without the protected health information. On Arbor Day, Ryker and Elyssa were discussing why the holiday slips by unnoticed, unless you're in elementary school.

"They need a sexier mascot," Ryker said. "Santa, Easter Bunny, Cupid, they all have sexy Halloween costumes available."

"I don't think I've seen a sexy Easter Bunny. Moving on, how would you make a tree sexy?" Elyssa asked.

"You've never seen one of them big booty bonsai?" Ryker opened Google. "Look at the junk in this trunk."

Later that night, Ryker sketched her proposed Arbor Day mascot.

"I stand corrected, Ryker, she's one hot oak." Elyssa laughed.

Halloween night, around 1600, Liam asked Ryker to come to his office over Teams. He praised her artistic talents and asked her if she had any Thanksgiving-themed art he could use for a personal project.

"Not to dissuade you, but all I've got are pin-ups or trippy land-scapes."

"Would you mind sending me one of each?" He raised his eye-brows.

Her flirty turkey spread her wings all over Drivers later that night. An immediate clue the invitation was not sanctioned by Drivers. Neither of them mentioned her drawing again. Ryker fully support-ed the slap in Human Resources' face, but she was disappointed Liam associated with the Pi Rats. He was too smart for their non-sense.

If they hadn't called Yvette and some of the others, cunts, it would've been a great presentation. Elyssa said she never saw him at any of their meetings. No one on the stage appeared to be a salaried employee. Maybe the managers and administrators convinced these idiots this was their opportunity to shine? Or they have the Pi Rat groups separated by pay-grade, and, as usual, the higher-paid people were more talk than action.

Unsure if Sunny would fill her in on the new plan, Ryker went to work on solving the murders. She'd been so distracted by the stuff in Eva's bag, she'd forgotten to complete step three, the timeline.

Using Fatima's Teams messages for Eva's inspection, and reasoning it had to be someone in the blood bank, Ryker narrowed her suspects down to four: Fatima, Liam, Dr. Sanders, and Quinneth. Dr. Sanders and Liam were in his office shortly after Desmund was found. Drivers Wednesday email blast removed Dr. Sanders from Dr. Kudela's timeline. A photo from the Director's Dinner supported his alibi; he stood front and center. Liam and Fatima passed the silver hand sanitizer test. No fucking way it's Quinneth.

A set of employee samples finished on her analyzer. First shift might have been too paranoid to look, unless a tech prints them, there's no way to track who clicked on what results. Like when Desmund came through the ER, high RDW usually has a mixed field flag. Why would vampires be any different?

Mixed field is caused by recent transfusion, stem cell transplant, or chimerism. The incidence rate of the last two was low. One sample displayed mixed field.

How am I going to know which samples belong to which employees?

The answer knocked on the stainless steel countertop of the blood bank service window.

Wearing a pink scrub top with a volunteer name tag on her chest, Sunny carried a purple lunch box cooler. Drivers logo barely visible under the "For biohazard only" sticker. This was the cooler they used to transport specimens during tube station downtime. Like the time a nurse failed to screw the lid on properly, did not seal the specimen bag, and sent a *C. diff* sample to the wrong lab with a broken carrier tube. All tube stations were down for hours while they decontaminated the system.

"Hey guys," Sunny smiled as she plopped the cooler onto the counter. "Who's ready for some ABOs?" she asked, making the cooler perform a little jig. "Can one of you let me inside?"

June opened the door.

"Volunteer?" Ryker asked, noting black scrub pants, an abnormal choice for Sunny.

"They emailed all the employees scheduled for orientation on Monday." Sunny continued to the sample processing area despite Ryker's eye roll.

"I choose to move on from how you got these samples," Ryker said aloud, but it was mostly for herself. She knew Sunny wasn't supposed to outright say she works for the SSB and they are running an operation. "There's only one sample showing mixed field. Is that our guy?"

"Oh, that's one possibility." Sunny closed the lid on the STAT centrifuge. "As a volunteer, I was told we also need to collect the samples with an O negative blood type. The others should be disposed."

"That doesn't make any sense. Vampires..."

Sunny interrupted, "Exnay on the ampirevay."

"Don't, they, directly, auto-transfuse, from, multiple, live, donors?" Ryker spoke as Sunny shook and nodded her head. "Of all the types, why would they be O neg?"

"Biologically, it makes more sense for them to be AB, universal recipients," Elyssa added.

Sunny's eyes scanned the room. "Are all the miscellaneous people gone?"

"It's the day before Thanksgiving. They left like an hour ago." Ryker said.

"Oh, well shit." Sunny ripped off the volunteer sticker. "Let's find us a fucking vampire."

Chapter 23

Current Day

"**Now do you understand** why I chose Sunny over you?" Felice didn't stretch, didn't yawn.

"Are you a robot?" The words flew out of Ryker's mouth. "Not like a sex robot. I mean, you could be, if you wanted. How are you so comfortable? We've been at this for what, six, six point five hours?"

"You were just about to stake your coworker."

Ryker leans forward, her chin hovering over the table, "If they removed you're brain and stuck it inside a robot, blink twice."

Wednesday: One Day Ago

As instructed, Ryker gathered the O negative samples. Elyssa retrieved three old patient samples from storage. One AB pos, one sample with a type discrepancy in the reverse, and one normal O neg sample.

Sunny separated the plasma and made a red cell suspension from each of the samples Elyssa brought her. "Using the non-employee as our negative control, I will first demonstrate what happens when you add O negative red cells to a tube with AB positive red cells while performing the classic immunohematology conjuration, the forward type."

"Too bad you didn't have time to add some choreography," Ryker said to Sunny's dramatic magician scientist.

When the twenty-second spin ended, Sunny removed the three glass tubes. "You there," she motioned to June, "Gaze, if you dare, into the agglutination mirror and tell the people what you see."

"I've always wanted to be chosen from an audience," June said, taking the tubes from Sunny. "I see four plus mixed field in all tubes."

"Round of applause for our lovely volunteer." Sunny waited until Ryker and Elyssa clapped.

June held out her labcoat and curtsied.

"We will now take a brief intermission to set the stage for our miracle. Snacks and beverages are available in the lobby. I recommend our Bloody Mary. I've just been told we're all out of Mary. It's now a Bloody Brenda. She's a spicy B pos who enjoyed long walks on the beach..."

"Sunny," Ryker cut her off, "We're finding a vampire."

"Ah, yes," Sunny cleared her throat. "Sorry, I got lost in character. I do need a few minutes before I call you guys back over."

Sunny separated the plasma from each suspect employee sample and placed it in a properly labeled glass tube.

The phone rang. June must have taken Sunny's suggestion to heart. Her labcoat hung on her chair, and she was not within visible range.

"Transfusion, this is Ryker...Let me check...Yes, I have an irradiation triage...Not approved...I'm sorry, did you see the comments...That makes sense, thanks."

"Questioning the Sandman?" Elyssa waved her finger.

"The patient came to the ER for abnormal labs," Ryker held the red cell order.

"That's not an indication."

"On its own, no. When the provider adds, possible leukemia, it is."

"Shit. What did Dr. Sanders say?"

"He said we'd honor it when they complete their diagnosis." Her spidey senses tingled. Maybe she could irradiate a short-dated unit, then June would have to use it and have a perfect cover story.

Four samples in, Sunny squealed as she read her tubes in the agglutination viewer. "Okay, you guys, intermission over."

They gathered around manual once more, including June, who returned from her personal intermission moments before the squeal.

"I need another volunteer, perhaps you, young miss." Sunny extended her arm to Elyssa. "Please have a seat. For this next scientific miracle, I would like you to drip a full forward and reverse type with this, sample of mystery."

Elyssa dripped one of the employee samples. Red cells with Anti-A, Anti-B, and Anti-D. Plasma with reagent A1 cells and B cells. Spin.

"Please tell us the forward type," Sunny smiled.

"O negative."

"And now...the reverse," Sunny emphasized reverse and mimed throwing a handful of snap pop fireworks to the ground with one hand and raised her other to the sky.

"It's all nonreactive, like it's AB plasma."

"Genius."

Ryker and June clapped on command.

The "I'm full" alarm sounded from the tube station. A singular tube landed at an odd angle and was stuck on the tube holding arm.

"Keep going," June said. "I don't want to throw off the vibes. The air is tingling."

"Ryker, will you come up on stage. This sample is historically A positive with an anti-A1, causing a type discrepancy. Will you please confirm those results?"

Ryker performed the test. The results were as expected; four plus, negative, four plus, two plus, four plus.

"Now, drip the reverse again. This time, I want you add an additional drop of normal AB plasma to the type discrepant plasma.

No change.

"A round of applause."

"That's it? I get the lame test?" Ryker protested.

"The spotlight has gone to this one's head." Sunny pointed at Ryker with her thumb.

Ryker rolled her eyes and moved out of the hot seat.

June returned for the finale.

"Let's recap. We've established combining normal O red cells with AB red cells causes a mixed field reaction. We've also established mixing AB plasma with type discrepant plasma does not change the results. My last miracle will be two-in-one. Watch what happens when I combine the testing of our A pos patient with the blood and plasma of the mystery sample."

Ryker could taste the anticipation. The centrifuge stopped.

"June, please read the forward type."

"A pos with mixed field in the A and D," June said. "Did I read this wrong?"

"You did not," Sunny said with enthusiasm. "The red blood cells from our mystery sample behave like normal human red blood cells. It's not that impressive yet, but soon it will be. Elyssa read the reverse."

Ryker squirmed. This was her investigation, and Sunny was giving away the coolest parts.

"No reactions!" It was the loudest Elyssa had ever spoken. "It's like an AB patient."

Sunny bowed. Another round of applause. "Before I leave to quest upon another miracle of nature, does anyone dare to guess whose sample this is?"

The lab door opened.

"Dr. Sanders," Ryker said.

"Ding, ding, ding. We have a winner." Sunny yelled into the pipette she held as a microphone.

"What do I win?"

Sunny dropped the pipette at his voice.

Dr. Sanders and his red plaid bow tie greeted them. "Is first shift gone already? I bet you all are thankful for that." He smiled, "I loved doing evenings. Daytime people are so stuffy."

He hoisted himself up to his spot on the sample prep bench. Next to him sat the mini biohazard bin they shoved wooden sticks into after reaming samples. He leaned over the bin and plucked out a pair with a large clot attached. He pinched the darkened slug between two wooden sticks like sashimi, then popped it in his mouth.

The room gagged. The slurp replayed directly in Ryker's throat as she struggled to catch her breath without vomiting.

"You're right," Dr. Sanders said, digging for another clotsicle. "Too much Wharton's Jelly. I told you, I'm not interested in neonates. Do we have any bad draws from the ER in here? The pain adds a depth you wouldn't believe."

The phone rang. No one moved.

"Go ahead and answer that," he said to June. "We're a trauma center, this could be an emergency."

"Blood bank, this is June...I can transfer you."

"Let me guess, a nurse called the blood bank to be transferred to the STAT lab instead of calling the STAT lab directly?"

June nodded.

"They've been doing that since they installed phones in hospitals. Isn't it funny how some things never change?" He put the bin back on the counter. "Speaking of, I remember changing our policy on issuing irradiated products. This is the only shift hell bent on ignoring that directive."

He dug around bare handed, like a kid in a tub of Halloween candy.

"I wouldn't do that if I were you," he said without looking up. "You, as in all of you. I can see the movement in your pockets. Ryker, please, you don't have to be a vampire to hear someone pressing buttons on the wan line. Let's go ahead and place all the cell phones in a biohazard bin."

They obeyed.

"Whose bright idea was it to give everyone irradiated blood and contaminate my food supply?"

Ryker raised her left hand. At this point, it was fifty-fifty whether or not Dr. Sanders attacked. Chopsticks at the ready, if he was going to swing, Ryker wanted it to be at her.

"I was hoping it was you. The way you challenge my decisions. Hearing my residents cry about you putting them in their place. In a few short months, you've permanently inserted yourself under Fatima's skin. That's amazing work."

Sunny stifled her laugh. The noise from her throat gained the crowd's attention, her cheeks flushed.

"The timeline doesn't fit. You weren't here when Dr. Kudela died. I saw you in Liam's office when Desmund came back into the ER."

"Desmund," Dr. Sanders salivated. "I did everything I could for that young man."

"You tore him into actual pieces."

"Let me explain. As Medical Director of Pathology, I spent years helping patients by lending my expertise. Blood bank consults, transfusion reaction investigations, please believe me, I tried to watch from a distance. I only interfered when I saw suffering. When I could smell death on their doorstep, I offered a more peaceful option."

"They were going to die anyway? That's your big defense?" Ryker couldn't stand this bullshit. "What about Desmund? Sickle cell disease doesn't have a long life expectancy, but he would have lived past twenty-four."

"He skipped his last exchange. Said he felt better and wanted to try to wean out of the exchange program. I made a house call. To reaffirm the need for his participation."

"That's horrifying," Elyssa shouted. "You stole his blood. You put him in crisis. The pain he experienced, the fear, the trauma. All for what? Your ego? So you could be his savior? That's sick."

"I took a chance on that young man, for his sake, to save him. If you had minded your own damn business and issued the exchange the way I told Fatima to do it, he'd still be alive." Saliva spewed from Dr. Sanders mouth as a spoke.

"Bullshit." Ryker, Elyssa, and Sunny said in a surprising unison.

"Horseshit," June added.

"Here's my offer," he continued in a more calming tone. "I want you on my team."

The lab door opened. Whoever Ryker hoped would walk through, this was not them.

Fresh red lipstick and bright pink eyeshadow made her features sharp, harsh. The disheveled hair and blood-stained business shirt gave full living dead vibes. The top buttons of her blouse were left open, exposing cleavage. The tail of her shirt flowed over one hip, and was partially tucked into the other. Her sleeved were rolled up to her elbows, revealing a tattoo Ryker couldn't quite make out. Eva embodied the nerd turned bad girl stereotype.

Dr. Kudela came in after. In life, he shadowed Dr. Sanders like a sad child at the zoo. In death, his role was the same.

How long were they standing at the door? Did they have a code word for their entrance cue?

"Hey, Sunny."

Chapter 24

BIRDS CHIRPED IN THE backyard below her balcony. It wasn't often Yvette got the house to herself. Her mom was out getting last-minute groceries for the family dinner. They couldn't have Thanksgiving without Hawaiian bread rolls.

The late afternoon sun warmed her face, her afternoon coffee warming her hands. Her favorite thing to do on days like this was to sit on her rocking chair and watch: the birds, the squirrels, the kids, the neighbors who are definitely having affairs.

Her phone vibrated with a text from Andy. She called him.

"Happy Thanksgiving," she said.

"Happy Thanksgiving," he responded. "Have you spoken to Ryker today?"

"No, I'm not in the lab. Why?"

"I sent her several texts. She hasn't responded."

"She is at work. She isn't supposed to be on her phone."

"Ha. Ha," Andy said. "She said some," he paused, "Odd things on Sunday. Did they tell you the CDC is here today, collecting employee samples? I think Ryker is planning something."

"It was in our group chat. Look, I'm worried about Ryker, too, but she's more than capable of taking care of herself. Her stress shows itself in ways we don't understand. We both know she won't open up if we keep pressing her. She needs space and time, she needs to feel like it was her choice."

"You think her stress is showing up as a vampire murder mystery?" He sounded doubtful.

"Vampires? She didn't mention vampires to me."

"Is there any way you can check on her without drawing suspicion? She might be getting herself into trouble."

"Actually, yes. Fatima didn't give me the on-call pager until yesterday afternoon. I left it in my labcoat on my door. I was trying to convince myself I didn't need it. Going to get it will remove my guilt about the pager, and your worry about Ryker. I'll text you when I get home to let you know how she's doing."

There was a surprise in her office she'd been hanging on to for Ryker. She considered giving it to her on Friday, but she didn't want it to feel forced. That wasn't her only hesitation. There's got to be a better way to show someone you trust them than gifting them a weapon?

Chapter 25

Wednesday: Eight Days Ago

THE BLACK ITALIAN ROAST burned as it came back up. He knew better than to have coffee on an empty stomach.

"What are your thoughts, Dr. Sanders?" Dr. Kudela beamed with enthusiasm this morning.

Dr. Sanders fought off a yawn as he replied, "It looks like the antibody formed the way antibodies do. We gave them a E positive unit, three days later, they made an allo Anti-E. The fever that occurred during the transfusion of the unit is consistent with the patient's other symptoms. Fever was coming and going throughout admission."

"But the blood bank didn't catch the big E with the transfusion reaction, they caught it 60 hours later with the new type and screen." Dr. Kudela said with a passion uncalled for this early in the morning.

"The techs followed their procedures. The tests did not indicate the need for further investigation. All we did was prove our practice of antibody screens every three days to be accurate. We aren't going to change our transfusion reaction procedure because we could have caught one antibody a little earlier. If we do that, we might as well make them order a new antibody screen after every blood transfusion, regardless of patient reaction. No one will agree to that. Besides, I want our policies to be consistent with AABB. A surprise inspection by the FDA is bad enough. Excessive type and screens is a good way to get CMS to accuse us of waste and fraud."

Kudela had a decent head on his shoulders. Great at recognizing problems. Not so great at solutions. He needed to learn the Drivers way of doing things. Understand how decisions can impact more than one patient. And, forget about the damn crystals.

Morning rounds cover a range of topics. After years as a teaching physician, Dr. Sanders settled on a preferred outline for the meeting. It starts with any major problems the resident from the night before encountered. A little bit of hot gossip to garner the interest of the voluntary participants: medical technologist students, and any rotating non-blood bank resident.

Once the audience is hooked, it's straight to business. Patients requiring transfusion consults, whether their provider asked for it or not. Each patient is discussed one at a time. Diagnosis, how that impacts their blood product consumptions, which blood products are indicated, and the logistics of getting those products.

"Moving on, we have two patients needing HLA matched platelets, one with a strong cold agglutinin. They are inducing labor today on a patient who requires washed red blood cells."

The last hour of the meeting is a learning game for the audience. The slide show of presentations past didn't garner the participation Dr. Sanders wanted. He was inspired by the game Dumb Ways to Die, and an insult he heard Ryker use during a staff meeting. He called it, "Unsmart Ways to Blood Bank."

He drafted scenarios from the irate emails written by his techs, forwarded to him from the blood bank director. After reading the situation, he offers the audience three options for what happens next. Then they try to guess which one occurred in real life. He liked to start the game with an example that tied into a patient they discussed that morning. Luckily, Ryker sent him the perfect situation a few months back.

"You're a transfusion resident. You have a patient with a strong cold agglutinin. The patient needs a blood warmer and a slow transfusion. This is your first time transfusing blood that requires a warmer. Do you A: Call the house supervisor to find a blood warmer? B: Ask the blood bank to warm up the unit by dunking it in the plasma thawer for a bit? C: Stock pile heel warmers from the NICU?"

One student says to the group, "There's no way they asked the house sup first. It wouldn't have made it into the game."

Once the anesthesiologist residents dropped their guard, they decided to choose the most ridiculous answer. Their train of thought, "As a blood bank resident, I would be aware of a plasma thawer and try to get the blood warmed as scientifically as possible."

The students countered with the heel warmers. One student adamant that blood warmers basically were bigger versions of heel warmers, "Like a big warm pillow."

"The answer was B." The residents cheered at getting the correct answer.

"Yes. I had a resident suggest they dunk the unit of blood in the plasma water bath. Luckily the tech was aware enough to inform the resident that was not an FDA approved option. The tech then suggested the resident have the nurse contact the house supervisor to help find a blood warmer." The students cheered when the lab tech held their ground. Learning together builds bridges and real world knowledge.

The noise of the blood bank threw him off balance this morning. *Is it always this loud and bright?* Head throbbing, stomach queasy. Getting through this day required a pick me up. There, in the bowl it's been in for weeks, Liam's homemade candies.

"Still not here? It's almost nine." Dr. Sanders pointed to his watch. The FDA inspector said they would be here first thing. "Do they think we can afford to wait around all day? Let me know when they arrive."

Liam nodded. Dr. Sanders pocketed another candy. Fatima caught him on his way out.

"Do you have a moment?" she asked.

He considered lying, saying he had another meeting, but her blood was perfumed with the spicy food she ate last night. He could savor the smell for a few minutes.

"I was just telling Liam about my concerns regarding our switch to Low Titer O Positive Whole Blood. Most studies don't account for survivor bias. The best paper they found to make their case, skewed the data to state that whole blood always has a better outcome than packed red blood cells. That has not been proven. Surely they don't have to use it on women of child bearing age. At least not until more studies are done? We've already given one young woman an anti-D. In one month we did what all the studies claim is highly unlikely."

"I understand, I have your emails. I anticipated having at least one person make an anti-D in the first year. When the books say it's unlikely, our patient population says *hold my beer*. Room temperature anti-C, anti-f, anti-Duffy three, anti-G. Hell, a warm auto antibody is an easy day for our techs. Yes, we've had one anomaly, but whole blood is the latest blood bank craze. It's making its way through all the major trauma centers. Life flights and ambulances around DFW have been equipped with it for nearly a year. Everyone is calling it a life saver."

"Well, I think we should keep a record, and report every anti-D after the whole blood to the FDA."

"I agree," Dr. Sanders said. In truth he didn't care. If it got her to leave him alone about a product he didn't have the power or willingness to change, she could send the FDA as many reports as she wanted. "Maybe you can ask them today if any other hospitals are doing the same thing. The more information they collect, the better."

This time of day was usually dedicated to responding to emails. No sense in changing his routine for an FDA inspector who couldn't bother to show up for business hours. One of the residents ate a bag of popcorn at their desk, another ate day old Glinda's. Residents ate breakfast like they were still undergrads. The smell from both seeped through the walls into his office. Not as pleasant as Fatima's spicy blood, but the fatty, greasy aromas caused him to drool.

His hunger ached to be satiated. He had to control himself with Desmund earlier that week. Not drain as much blood as he wanted. He thought he could scare him into compliance with Driver's sickle cell program. Alas, all it did was cause Desmund to double down on his mistrust of Drivers. If Desmund wanted to ignore his treatment and die an early death, Dr. Sanders could help with that. Besides, he couldn't have the word demon floating around his infusion clinic.

His pager sounded, "Mandatory meeting in ten minutes. See email."

It was an abuse of the paging system. However, it was better than getting dozens of text messages replying, "ok," to system wide upper management group threads. The word mandatory didn't sit well with him, either. As a doctor, the only thing mandatory was patient care. These pencil pushers weren't saving lives, but they sure as hell could make young doctors believe they were. They paid the bills. When it wasn't too inconvenient, Dr. Sanders joined the mandatory meetings.

A minute after the page, he got a text from Liam, "The inspector is at the hospital services desk."

"Go ahead without me," he replied. "We've got a mandatory meeting. I'll let them know you are unable to attend. I'll find you afterwards."

He logged into desktop. "If you're able, I would like everyone to turn on their video feed." The hospital CEO requested. Faces of board members, directors, and chiefs opened like the intro to the Brady Bunch.

"It's been brought to my attention there is a developing fraction, fraction is a strong word. A subset of employees who have joined the pirate, excuse me, Pi Rat, movement. We are a public, county hospital. Displays of political affiliation are prohibited on campus. As you all know, our Holiday Committee planned a special Thanksgiving event. We expected some push back. Those employees don't represent everyone. It's my firm belief they do not represent the majority. What I need from you is a united front. We need to show our support for this dinner, and what it stands for. I refuse to pretend this event didn't happen. This dinner is what the board agreed upon.

For our community and for our employees we lost, they deserve remembrance."

Two hours of group discussion for the best way to identify a Pi Rat. Then half an hour of everyone in the meeting serving platitudes and plaudits before they were dismissed. If the meeting were an email, his alerts would be going off for the rest of the day with hyperbolic declarations of leadership. At least this way he only had to hear it once. Dr. Sanders wondered if the CEO felt the same way. There's only so many fake compliments you can hear in a day before they make your skin crawl.

Speaking of, Dr. Kudela sent him a text message, "Your door was closed so I didn't want to knock, but when you get a moment can I ask you about that transfusion reaction from last night? I'm finalizing my report now."

Dr. Sanders appreciated straightforward communication. He didn't need all the please and thank yous. The assumption is all requests are voluntary. All questions are welcome so long as they aren't asked in malice.

"That looks adequate. By the way, adequate is what we aim for in medical notes. This isn't entertainment. I would add a sentence stating the patient is eligible for further transfusions at this time. If you don't add that, you'll get at least three phone calls asking for that exact clarification."

His phone vibrated with a text from Liam. "Fatima is with Eva, our FDA inspector, in the conference room looking over our policies."

"Dr. Kudela, come with me to greet our inspector," Dr. Sanders said.

"I still need to finish my consult." Dr. Kudela's eyes widened.

"Yes, you do. This is also important. It's easy nowadays to be a medical director behind closed doors. This could be my years speaking, but in my experience departments run better when you are thought of as a person, not some ghoul who pops out of thin air to yell then vanish into the darkness."

He saw the light glisten off something in the inspectors hand sanitizer bottle as she tucked it back into her bag. His hand warmed at her touch. He held on a few seconds longer, to see if she would notice the rise in temperature. His resident's tongue greeted the room from the side of his mouth. Had they not been in the room in together, the family resemblance might have gone unnoticed.

Vampire skin is wildly sensitive. Hell, even sun light burns. It's not a dramatic spontaneous combustion, but it isn't comfortable. Humans have been protecting their skin from the sun for as long as they've been exposed to it. The zinc oxide, oils, and pastes from his vampire youth have transformed into convenient SPF bottles. These liquid physical barriers also offer protection from other skin sensitivities. Like the silver in Eva's hand sanitizer.

How exciting.

It had been years since the last time he was hunted. A battle before the bite made the blood taste richer, and damn he was hungry.

Chapter 26

Wednesday: One Day Ago

"**Hey, Sunny,**" **Eva said** with a big, shit-eating grin.

"Nevasha?" Sunny's voice trembled. "I thought you were on vacation?"

"I was. Now it's permanent. I came here to prove the clinical existence of vampires. To show Felice I deserved more, I could do more. I thought the SSB was everything. Felice never believed in me. Dr. Sanders has a plan for us. I think you'll love it."

"You just listed so many teams. Which one are we joining?" June asked.

"It means becoming a fucking vampire." Nevasha retorted.

"Geeze. Okay, already." Ryker said.

"Okay!" Sunny screamed. "Ryker, I cannot let you volunteer for that."

"Oh, sorry," Ryker said. "I didn't understand the whole team thing. We already work for the guy. I meant *okay* as in, I get it now."

"You're turning down my offer?" Dr. Sanders tapped his fingertips together.

"I'm telling you to shove your offer up your deflated ass." Ryker held her chopsticks for the room to see. June and Elyssa pulled theirs out. After the chaos of the dinner, Elyssa was more upset that Ryker hadn't warned them to carry weapons than she was about the vampire accusation.

Sunny drew a wooden stake from her pocket. "I don't want to fight you."

Nevasha lunged at Sunny and tossed her aside like a throw pillow, "You won't have to." She smiled, "Don't worry, your friends will only be dead until sunrise. Then we can all be besties. Every night can be girls' night."

Sunny lay limp after hitting the edge of the workbench.

Dr. Kudela remained close to the door. Dr. Sanders lifted himself back to his viewing spot. He held the mini biohazard bin like a bag of popcorn.

Ryker, June, and Elyssa gathered around Sunny. She moaned as she struggled to her feet.

"I don't think we can fight them." Sunny clutched her wrist.

"G units at the ready."

On Ryker's command, Elyssa dug in her pocket, pulling out a side container of garlic dipping sauce. Dr. Sanders popped a stick in his mouth, licked it clean, then chucked it into the bin with their phones.

Nevasha took three steps closer, then gagged on the garlic-filled air. Dr. Sanders laughed as she forced herself to continue. As soon as she was in range, Ryker fired first, hitting Nevasha square in the chest with the back of the container. Dr. Sanders nearly fell off the workbench when the sauce spilled onto the floor.

Elyssa tossed hers, direct hit to the face. Nevasha covered her mouth with her hand and hunched forward. Her cheeks puffed. Dark reddish-brown liquid trickled between her fingertips onto the floor. Her jaw moved up and down like she was trying to swallow it.

While Nevasha's head was down. Ryker stepped forward again. The barf bomb erupted. Ryker evaded the puke waterfall and squirted hand sanitizer down the side of Nevasha's face and neck.

Flesh dissolved on the areas of bare skin exposed to the silver. She writhed in pain, falling with her back on the floor. Blood gargled in her throat. Her body flinched with each attempted breath.

Chopsticks aimed, Elyssa went in for the kill strike.

"Naahaaa," Ryker moaned. She wanted to shout, "Not yet. I think it's a trap," but there wasn't enough time.

In one swift movement, Nevasha grabbed Elyssa by the ankle, Elyssa fell on top of her, and Nevasha clamped down on her neck. Ryker and Sunny pulled at Elyssa's limp shoulders, Nevasha wouldn't let go.

"Nevasha, please," Sunny screamed. "You don't have to do this. We can help you."

Elyssa thunked to the side, landing on her back. She wasn't bleeding. Her body couldn't bleed. Nevasha drained it all. She licked the blood around her mouth as she moved to her hands and knees.

"One down." Then to Sunny, "You want to help me? Tie your hair up." Nevasha leaned against the shelves under the workbench to regain her feet. She wobbled. New, bright pink dermis covered her once-exposed jawbone; she was healing.

This wasn't part of the plan. None of this was part of the plan. Three vampires?

Each step Nevasha took towards them, she regained more strength. Each time her foot hit the off white, worn-down tile, she looked less human and more like a predator stalking its prey.

"Quick, I have an idea," Sunny said. "Buy me some time."

Someone else's hand reached into Ryker's pocket, then it left. No time for fledging any plan. Ryker had just connected the dots on Sunny's auditory input when she found herself standing face to healed face with Nevasha. How could she stall a vicious killer without getting herself killed?

"Some people say we look alike."

"What?" Nevasha asked.

"From the back."

"I don't..." The hunt faded from her eyes.

"Our hair. The donut bun. People on first shift thought I was supposed to be killed, but they got you by mistake."

"That's so goddamn stupid."

"Right? The only person dumb enough to do that is," to her surprise, Nevasha finished the statement with her, "Quinneth."

"Pinch, poke, you owe me a Coke." Nevasha turned to Dr. Sanders. "B T Ws, you have to fire that Quinneth girl. She's a liability waiting to happen. I didn't include it in my report, but I saw her load the wrong lot number of screening cells on the machines. I asked her if it was normal to have more than one set on the machine at a time. She told me she does it to avoid delays in reloading reagents. She also said as long as the machine had QC for the day, it would work no matter what lot number you used."

"I fucking knew it!" Ryker yelled, validation fueling her soul.

"Yeah," Nevasha said to Ryker. "Then, I wanted to catch Fatima in a lie, so I moved all the current lot to a random fridge in the back. I wanted her to tell me all normal processes were followed to change lot numbers. She's got a lead foot for gaslighting."

"That was you?" Ryker asked. "That didn't faze Fatima. All it did was make her think I'm some defensive dickhead." She felt something drop into her pocket.

"I can't take all the credit for that. You've put in so much work on your own."

Distraction over. Ryker threw a right hook. It landed.

Sunny pounced. She used Ryker's momentum to press Ryker down, and Sunny leapfrogged onto Nevasha. Nevasha went for the kill bite. She recoiled. Her lips and tongue melting. With one forearm around Nevasha's neck, Sunny reached back and drove a stake through her heart.

Nevasha let out a primal scream before falling to the ground.

"One down," Sunny said.

"Hand sanitizer on the neck?" Ryker asked.

Sunny nodded.

"Dr. Kudela, would you please clean up the mess your sister made?" Dr. Sanders asked.

Fangs descended, tongue out, Dr. Kudela headed towards the group.

"June, we need your sauce," Ryker said.

June shook her head, "I used it."

"What? When?" Ryker didn't take her eyes off Dr. Kudela as he approached. "There's only two cups on the floor?"

"I had it for a snack."

Dr. Sanders let out another full belly laugh, "And y'all shuddered at my choice of appetizer."

"I had bread," June advocated. "I didn't know we would need it today."

On a wire shelf set up to house the gel cards for the new instruments, lay an unnecessarily large box cutter. When Liam ordered them for the lab, he said he thought it was average-sized.

Ryker scolded herself for not grabbing it earlier. Dr. Kudela didn't miss it. Blade unsheathed, cutter held high in the air, an OSHA nightmare. Ryker tugged on Elyssa's feet, desperate to move her away from the approaching vampire. Dr. Kudela swung his arm. Ryker closed her eyes and shielded Elyssa. She waited for the blood to trickle, for the air to reach the exposed nerves, for the pain. She was fine.

Kneeling over his sister, Dr. Kudela stared at her decapitated body. "If you don't cut off the head," he said through sobs. "They can come back. The stake is temporary. The head is permanent." He held his sister's hand. "All this time, she thought I was searching for the vampire who killed our mom. I never told her I found him. He didn't just kill her, he turned her. Mom visited for a while. She told me everything. Told me about his stupid socks and bow tie. One night, she said the blood lust grew too strong, it wasn't safe for her to come back. I was searching for a cure.

"The irradiated blood was helping. The crystals diminished after transfusion. I told Eva not to come here. I told her I wasn't ready. She thought the irradiation was just a deterrence. If I could figure out how irradiation prevented turning, maybe I could use it to make an antidote. Desmund, with sickle cell disease, he would have made it if it weren't for..."

"Me," Dr. Sanders said, picking fibrin from his teeth with a fingernail. "If I knew your mom would turn out to be a self-hating vampire, I would've let her stay dead. She fed off rats and squirrels. Even the lives of poor rodents were too much for her to take. She jumped out of a tree with razor wire around her neck." He hopped off the counter. "I told your sister you weren't a good fit for us. But nooooo, she made a promise to protect you. She wanted to be your big sister forever. What a waste. She was the only Deluka willing to accept the vampire's true nature."

Oh my god," Ryker said. This whole time she'd been basing the timeline off of a single vampire. Now that she knew there were three, the solution came to her like an eluate turning blue when it reaches the correct pH. "Your sister. She killed Desmund."

"Yes." Dr. Kudela closed his eyes and nodded, a tear falling down his cheek. "Not just him."

Ryker gasped, "No. That's how Dr. Sanders was at the dinner when you died. He didn't kill you, either. Your sister did."

"She said she wanted..."

Crwwwwrrck. Dr. Kudela's head lifted off his neck. His body rolled to the floor next to his sister's.

"He was annoying. Always going on about how great his sister is, then he kills her. For what? Between you and me, his research was pointless." Dr. Sanders smiled. "The world doesn't need a Plan B for vampires. The world needs more vampires. And what's with the tongue thing?" Dr. Sanders strummed Dr. Kudela's side-stuck-out tongue like a cat playing with a door stopper. Blood trickled gently from Dr. Kudela's severed neck. Dr. Sanders slung the head into the wall of blood refrigerators. He licked the remnants of Dr. Kudela off his fingers. "The original plan, if you wanted to know, was for me to turn just you, Ryker. It was going to be my Secret Santa gift. Then

Nevasha came along, and I thought *how great would it be to have one big Vampire Thanksgiving?*"

"I don't do family gatherings." Ryker stood within arm's reach of Dr. Sanders. She knew that meant he was within arm's reach of her, but if there was a chance Elyssa was still human, she wasn't going to let Dr. Sanders change that.

"You're protecting her." He tilted his head, "Adorable. But you're too late, I can smell her changing. Not even precious irradiated blood could save her now. She'll be one of us in the morning."

The door alarm from one of the fridges sounded. Dr. Kudela's head must've knocked it open.

Dr. Sanders grimaced, "Someone mute that wretched alarm."

"Is the loud noise hurting your sensitive ears?" Sunny asked, inching towards the row of refrigerators.

"Turn the damn thing off."

"Make me," Sunny dared, prompting the alarm activation on another fridge.

"Nothing but defiance from all of you."

Slap. While Dr. Sanders yelled at Sunny, Ryker dipped her hand in the garlic puddle from her first throw. When he turned back to emphasize you, she slapped him.

He took her by the forearm, "You think garlic will protect you from me?" He leaned into her face, "I'll save you for last, so you can watch all your friends become monsters."

"Hey," Ryker dug in her pocket with her loose hand. "I have more than three friends." It took her longer than she wanted to find the hand sanitizer. She'd trained her entire career for this next move. She freed the bottle from her pocket, flicked the lid open with her thumb, and squeezed as hard as she could to empty its contents.

The bottle farted pellets of silver liquid.

Dr. Sanders leaned his head back, "It's been such a long time since I've laughed this hard. I'll try not to kill your sense of humor with your humanity."

He dug into Ryker's neck, his teeth breaking her skin. It burned. It burned like she was touching the oven. She couldn't flinch. She wanted to flinch. Why wasn't she flinching? Then it stopped. Her ass landed on Eva's decapitated head.

"Ryker, are you ok?" Sunny called, rushing to her side.

Dr. Sanders turned to display the stake sticking out of his back. He stepped towards the counter, placed one hand palm up on his forehead, then collapsed.

"Now what?" Ryker asked, cupping the wound on her neck.

"I need to make a phone call," Sunny said. "Anyone willing to get our cells out of the biohazard?"

The lab door opened. Everyone, alive, screamed.

Yvette screamed back at them.

"Thank god it's you," Ryker said.

"I'm not here," Yvette rushed, "I'm not on the clock." She disappeared into her office without taking a first or second glance at the bodies lying on the floor.

Sunny stepped into the empty office to call the *CDC*. That left Ryker with June to contemplate what the fuck happened in the last few minutes. The headless siblings lay next to each other. Elyssa hadn't moved. No rise and fall of breath. Ryker took her temperature with their infrared thermometer. Thirty degrees Celsius. She was gone. Ryker knew what she had to do next.

The phone rang.

"Transfusion, this is Ryker...Did we get your blood request?" A familiar alarm sang from the front of the lab. "It might be in our tube station, we were," she didn't know what to say, "In a meeting with our medical director. If I don't have it, I'll call you back."

"Are you working? Are we supposed to work? After all this?" June wafted her hand around the quadruple homicide.

"I can't do anything else. I can't bring Elyssa back. I can't superglue vampire heads. You do what you want, I'm going to do my best to ensure no one else dies tonight."

Something moved out of the corner of her eye. A hand? A finger?

Ryker motioned to June to be quiet and move to the office with Sunny. When June was clear, she tapped Dr. Sanders's calf. His foot slid out from under him as he rolled off the counter. Gravity took him to the floor, but he stopped. His left arm stiffened and held his body weight in a plank position.

"What the hell?" Ryker whispered.

"That was a close one," Dr. Sanders said as he stood, reaching back in a double-jointed circus-performing nightmare. "Not quite deep enough." He tossed the chopsticks to the side. "This is when you run."

"Shiiiiit," Ryker let out as she dashed for Yvette's office. She was at the door when he caught her arm.

"Nighty, night," Fangs snarled, mouth agape.

Tinkslllppppsplink.

Dr. Sanders paused, tilting his head. Her pizza slices and space cats lanyard lay centered between Ryker's feet. His grasp eased for a moment, and Ryker seized it to free herself.

He laughed. Head back. Deep and boisterous. "Stubborn med techs. There is no escape. You will all die tonight."

Siiirrriiiiich.

His eyes went dull. A sharpened broom handle protruded from his chest. His arms hung loose at his sides, his head bobbed as the extra-large wooden stake bounced up and down before it all fell to the floor.

"One thing about Drivers I could never stomach," Yvette said from her threshold. "All the damn vampires."

Chapter 27

Current Day

"**YVETTE DID NOT SAY** that. That is poor misuse of a line from a movie."

"First of all, you weren't there. The quote is canon. Second of all, you know The Lost Boys? I grew up on that movie. If you've seen The Monster Squad, I might be in love with you."

"Let's back up a little."

"I might be in like with you."

"I told you not to lie." Felice's face stone cold.

"Where's the lie." Ryker re-traced her story.

"There is no way you have more than three friends," Felice says. Not a hint of laughter.

Long pause.

"Was that a joke? Did you sell your soul for knowledge and power, and the demon who took it forces you to make one joke a day at sunrise?" Ryker waits for correction. "That was hurtful."

"Which is more painful, only having three friends, or putting a stake through one of them?"

Ryker locks eyes with Felice. Concentrating, she visualizes her left eyebrow raising in an arch, mirroring Felice. "Am I doing it?"

"If by *it* you mean scrunching your face into a myriad of moronic expressions? Yes. It's time for you to finish."

"Yes, ma'am." Ryker gives up on the single lift and offers Felice a strong double pump. "That was pretty much it. Yvette saved the day. Sunny told us not to cut off Dr. Sanders's head because of some stupid lie about CDC bullshit. You really should give her a list of specific cover stories. We're scientists, we ask good questions. Any-who, Elyssa was dead. I staked her through the heart so she wouldn't surprise attack anyone when she had her blood lust awakening."

"Why did Yvette show up?"

"She's the supervisor on call this week. Left the pager in her office."

"She just happened to have a giant wooden stake with her?"

"Bristley Spears is always at work," Ryker says, with a poor attempt at voguing her arms.

"What did you do in the time between staking your friend and us...."

A knock on the door interrupts Felice.

Darkness. It registered as darkness, yet she could see. The rises and folds in the fabric glowed like a mountain range backlit by a stunning dark blue sky. The metal zipper glimmered, the river flowing through this beautiful landscape.

No fear. No pain. The ache in her neck that taunted her until her last breath, gone. Last human breath. Elyssa felt the automatic rise of her lungs.

Weird.

She lay and counted her breaths. Three per minute.

A strong odor emanated from her right. To her left, she felt a presence, not stinking of death, not alive. As if the body were on pause. A wave of sadness culminated in her chest. A couple centimeters to the left, and Elyssa would be in the same state as her fellow passenger.

The chopsticks formed a makeshift tent under the navy fabric. Noticing an odd sensation, Elyssa reached for her hip. A clump of money fell out of the yellow-lined paper someone tucked into her underwear.

Elyssa laughed as she placed the note and assorted bills into her scrubs pocket.

She'd have to get a new cell phone, her driver's license, and bank cards. Then she could cash out and hide. Scott made her his beneficiary when they got engaged. His family insisted she take the insurance money. The guilt she carried in life, now irrelevant in her life after death. Forget Lexapro. Becoming a vampire cured her human mental health issues in a single sunrise.

The van stopped. Elyssa didn't know their exact location. The air smelled of cow.

⊘⊘⊘

"What did you do in the time between staking your friend and us..."

A knock on the door interrupts Felice mid-sentence. *Somebody better be dead.* Ryker's jaw opens wide, expelling yet another yawn into the stuffy conference room. *Girl needs to learn how to cover her mouth.*

The agent stands directly in the doorway, preventing her from exiting. Another is near the far wall, back to Felice.

"Ma'am, there's an emergency we need to discuss."

She waits. If something is emergent enough to interrupt her interrogation, it certainly shouldn't need her prompting to hear it.

"Pro tip," Ryker shouts from her chair. "If she doesn't respond, it's because she's pissed." There's a pause. "Or delighted."

Felice closes the door. "She's not wrong."

"Yes, Ma'am," said the mid-twenties man. Tall, pale, with long dark hair tied into a bun. "There was an issue with the van at a rest stop outside Oklahoma City..."

As anger rises in her body, Felice redirects the energy into maintaining her poise and breath. *That little asshat in the conference room thinks she can play me for a fool.*

$$\mathcal{O}\mathcal{O}\mathcal{O}$$

"I'M SORRY I WAS an asshole during the dinner, and in general, really," Ryker said.

"Apology accepted for the dinner," Elyssa said. "Don't stop being an asshole at work. I was the asshole at my previous workspace. It gets lonely, but someone needs to do it. You can't gentle parent incompetence. Give me a few more months, I'll be an asshole with you."

"Thanks. I needed that. And thank you for believing me about the vampire. Andy thought I was going crazy."

"Why can't we have both?" Elyssa joked. "Besides, a vampire hunt is an amazing way to disassociate. It's terrifying, but how cool would it be if vampires were real? I'm not saying I want to be a vampire, but I'm not a definite no." She leaned against the black worktop and watched Ryker fill in her soft lines with patterns.

"Aren't you worried you'd enjoy murdering people and become evil?" Ryker asked.

"Nope. Never considered that. However, if I do join the dark side, I give you permission to take me out."

"Deal," Ryker said.

"What about you? What would you want?" Elyssa asked. The expression on her face one of genuine curiosity.

"We'll leave that up to my chaos demon," Ryker said. "The drawings keep her happy." She filled in a random oval with lines, then added, "If I do get turned, don't let Sunny's people take me and do experiments on me."

"Deal, but I don't want to be a lab puppet either."

Ryker turns that conversation and all her current thoughts on Elyssa into little bubbles. She watches as they lift from her head and drift into the clouds above Drivers.

Felice is taking forever. Boredom sinks in. Ryker spins her chair in circles until her body reminds her that's a game for the youth. She stands, clasping her hands behind her back and releasing the tension in her shoulders. Breathing in the potential lie to force her heart rate to accept it as reality, and exhaling the truth to disappear into the wind, or HVAC system.

Felice re-enters the conference room. "Look at this," she says, holding a phone.

"That is not a safe parking spot." Ryker tisks. In the picture, a familiar white van was somehow lodged into the sparse, brown leaf canopy of a solid tree. Cows grazed in the background pasture, a picturesque southern Whomping Willow. "I've regarded the image. Please give me further instructions."

Felice swipes. "Do you notice anything wrong with this photo?" She raises her voice, but manages to decrescendo by the end of her question.

"Wrong or missing?" Ryker pretends to give it a solid review. "Someone disobeyed what I can only assume were your orders and disconnected the Sandman's head. So his body is missing, but morally, he deserved it."

"You don't know anything about this?"

"No?" It felt honest. She had no idea what Elyssa was going to do when she woke up as a vampire.

"You don't sound sure."

"You didn't ask specific." Ryker audibly draws a deep breath. "I know the van. I knew Dr. Sanders. I assumed you put the bodies somewhere. I know heads usually have a person attached."

"Where's Elyssa?"

"If she's not in the van in the tree, then I have no idea. I've been in here with you all night." That last sentence wasn't needed. It would only raise suspensions. What could they do? It wasn't her fault they didn't make sure the chopsticks went all the way through the center of Elyssa's heart. She thanked Dr. Sanders for that idea.

Felice glares, her deep brown eyes burrowing through Ryker's soul. It's so intense, Ryker is afraid to move. She thinks about winking again or blowing a kiss. Neither of those options ended with Ryker having all of her teeth.

"You think you've won. You think you outsmarted me. You'll mess up. Elyssa will mess up. When I find her, I'm going to personally remove her fangs with rusty pliers and send them to you. Don't worry, they'll grow back. You'll know she's dead when you stop getting my mail."

Ryker stifles a laugh. "I'm sorry. I know you're serious." She tucks her head down, "Please don't hit me. The whole thing sounded terrifying until you threatened the annoying metal box I have to empty once a month. But, yes. Threat made. Point taken."

The way Felice stares back at Ryker, pure loathing. Ryker wonders if that's how she looks to Quinneth during turnover.

Felice leaves the room once more.

After a few minutes of silence, Ryker mumbles the song that's been playing in her head since she inadvertently said the inspirational sentence.

Vamps in the van, and the van in the tree, and the tree in the hole, and the hole in the ground, and the green grass grows all around all around, and the green grass grows all around.

Chapter 28

Monday: Three Blood Bank Days Later

"I'VE GOT TWO UNITS in here for you," Regina said as she slid the apheresis cooler off her cart and onto the blood bank window counter. "Did you hear about Dr. Sanders?"

"I've heard Dr. Sanders is no longer an employee at Drivers. He has no privileges at this facility or any Drivers affiliate. Even Liam's lips are tight about the whole thing." Ryker checked the unit's temperature; two point six Celsius.

"You didn't hear this from me." Regina leaned forward, "According to the STAT lab, Dr. Kudela was collecting data on patients while Dr. Sanders was doing some sort of experiment on them. That fake FDA lady, that was Dr. Kudela's girlfriend. First she has a stroke, less than a week later Dr. Kudela has one, and now Dr. Sanders has vanished. It all seems real suspicious."

"No shit." Ryker tore off the ziptied crossmatch tag and tucked it into the paperclip holding the pickup request.

"They pay Dr. Sanders so much money, tell us how big and important he is. He's gone. We're still here. Still working. Like nothing happened. Let that be a reminder to all of us. Be grateful for the job, but be more grateful for yourself." She nodded her head and left.

Ryker was plenty grateful to not be in some weird Specialists in Supernatural Beings jail. Assuming they have one. She waited in the conference room for what seemed like another hour for Felice to come back. She paced the room, did table push-ups, lunges, anything to keep herself awake. She might not win, but she'd put up a fight if they tried to take her.

When the door eventually opened, Ryker popped out of her seat.

The environmental services worker clutched his chest, "I'm sorry, I thought the room would be empty." He held a white styrofoam container. Syrup and bacon perfumed the air.

"No problem. I think I fell asleep for a second. What time is it?" Ryker asked.

"Eight-thirty," he said, confused. "I can leave."

"No, I apologize for startling you. It's time for me to go. Enjoy your breakfast."

Ryker went to her locker for her keys and work bag. Her phone sat on top. June retrieved them from the biohazard bins. The black scrubs made her store it before handcuffing her to the chair in the breakroom.

Yvette worked with Ryker and June through the holiday. At the SSB's request, they told Liam that Elyssa left early Wednesday night. Monday afternoon, he asked Ryker if she'd heard from her.

"She was upset after the dinner, she didn't appreciate the second part of the slide show," Ryker said loud enough for Malia to overhear.

A tube fell, pulling Ryker back into the moment. A request for blood. Name, date of birth, medical record number, product, nurse employee ID, nurse phone number. Damn, they put the wrong tube station.

"Hi, this is Ryker in transfusion. I have a request for blood on patient Spencer...you wrote tube station 668...No, that's the tube station for the STAT lab...No, that's my tube station...You think that's the number or you're certain that's the number...Is there someone you can ask...240...Give me a moment to confirm." Ryker put the phone down and tried the numbers, nine observation appeared as the destination.

When she picked up the phone, someone in the background yelled, "You read every number on the screen except our tube station."

"Yes, I will send it to 240," she said into the receiver. "It happens. Thanks."

After sending the unit, Ryker pulled up a tab in Chrome, "How to send someone money without the government tracking?" She knew they were watching her. She already found two listening devices hidden in her apartment. She also spent the weekend driving to Austin to buy a new phone, in person, which she set up herself. The distance wasn't necessary. She figured the SSB might think Elyssa was hiding out in her hometown.

The Google searches were for fun. She had a whole story planned out.

"How to replace a driver's license online."

"How to live off the grid."

"Best Bloody Marys in San Antonio."

"Is it illegal to take expired blood from a blood bank?"

She browsed blood bank employment listings. It was a semi-regular search for her. Maybe the SSB would assume vampire Elyssa could no longer use computers, and she needed Ryker's help hunting for a new job.

In truth, she had no idea where or what Elyssa was doing. While Sunny was on the phone with the "CDC," Ryker scrounged together all the paper money she could find. She kept a hundred-dollar bill in her wallet for emergencies, and took the cash from the communal-supplies envelope.

"Elyssa the Vampire sounds so lame," Ryker wrote. "I hope you wake up before they find this letter. Otherwise, we might be seeing each other sooner than either of us wants. I wasn't trying to be creepy with the stripper money. I thought they might search you before tossing you into a white van, but they probably wouldn't undress you until they got to wherever you're going.

"I left your phone in the biohazard. It was too suspicious to dig it out for a dead person, and it had the most blood on it. Also, trackers and whatnot. I know I didn't show it often, but I enjoyed working with you. You're a good tech. Whatever you do, please don't come back to Drivers. I know they will force Sunny to keep an eye on me, and who knows how many agents they'll have looking for you once you make your escape.

"If it's possible, could you do something with your new vampire superpowers so I know you made it? You better be a fucking vampire or I'm going to feel guilty about putting chopsticks in your chest and not calling 911. Try not to murder innocent people. Maybe you could be a vigilante vampire and kill other murderers or people who drive under the speed limit in the fast lane?

"TLDR. Good luck, and don't fuck it up."

Chapter 29

"PASCAL? JE SUIS LA."

The black and white French Bulldog lifted his head from a pile of pillows, yawned, and stretched. Leaving his belly exposed for much-needed rubs.

Liam obliged. After all, poor Paspup has been home alone all day while Liam was off keeping the blood bank from collapsing in on paperwork. Two weeks ago, he promised himself the long hours would only be temporary. He would make time for the important things, like belly rubs, and the reintroduction of supernatural beings into the modern world.

Late one evening, after his second rum and Dr. Pepper, Liam perused Pinterest for fun dessert ideas. He stumbled across a post titled, "Dracula Candy."

The original poster, Gladson45896, claimed this tasty treat would be yummy enough for any vampire to sink their teeth into. Gladson45896 also listed several renditions of carrot cake, sourdough bread, and casseroles, all low potassium and garlic-free, for those with sensitive stomachs.

The recipe was simple: Diet Coke, water, sugar, and fresh blood. A note from the creator assured the audience this was a joke. They further explained the humor and patted themselves on the back for their cleverness. An asterisk suggested a drop or two of pig's blood per candy would be enough to satisfy your vampire friends without grossing out your human guests.

Liam had not suspected anyone in his lab was a vampire, but he needed something to spruce up the mundane task of blood bank manager. He added five drops of blood to each one-inch circle mold.

Sitting in a matching red candy dish on the corner of his desk. He counted the candies every day and the people who took them. Only one person came back for more.

The night of the FDA inspection, when Dr. Sanders came to Liam's office to discuss their performance, he reached for the candy. Dr. Sanders smiled as he twisted the wrapper open. A tiny smear of blood appeared on his left canine.

Acknowledgements

I want to thank everyone who read Tales from Transfusion: The Inclusion. I love murder mysteries. The Thanksgiving episodes of Bob's Burgers are my absolute favorite. I always imagined this as if those two things had a book baby. A third novel in this series is in the works.

I'd also like to thank my coworkers for the continued inspiration.

Lastly, to all my friends who volunteer for conversations that involve me giving them very little context for a scene, them throwing their solutions at me, me rejecting all of them, landing on my own solution, then thanking them for their help. You can look forward to more of those.

About the Author

Marlene is a ten year Medical Laboratory Scientist. She graduated from York College of Pennsylvania with a Bachelor of Science in Biology. She earned her post-graduate certification in Clinical Laboratory Science from Texas Tech University Health Science Center, back when it was called the School of Allied Health.

The point of this series is to introduce people to the career of laboratory medicine, and hopefully give them a laugh or two along the way. She enjoys long walks in the woods, tending to her houseplants, cats and monster trucks.

Her instagram and tiktok are @MsMarleneTower.

As always, if you enjoyed the book, please pass it to a friend. If you think it's trash, leave a copy in your breakroom.

www.ingramcontent.com/pod-product-compliance
Lightning Source LLC
Chambersburg PA
CBHW022145170626
46807CB00005B/2078